"Allan! You feel so good!"

"So do you," I said.

Again our lips met and, still holding the kiss, I drew her to a reclining position on the sofa. What followed was tensely exciting and I forgot that I didn't love Ruby. Deeper and deeper I fell into her encircling passion, and bolder and bolder came her reciprocation to my ardent caresses.

Time became suspended. Nothing was urgent. But at the same moment I knew of two people lost in a great pool of furious emotion, Ruby and myself. Things were happening and I wasn't sure I was one of the two at the controls. Regardless of my lack of experience, the whole thing was like second nature, an instinct which guides one through the darkness.

The catch came, the possible trap, when minutes later I discovered the absence of disgust I'd previously felt after such intimacy. There was a gnawing hunger lurking in my heart, and I was holding Ruby more tightly than anytime before. It was like when you get up from the table still hungry, and you're reluctant to leave anything behind. So, I continued to hold her, nestling my cheek against hers.

BEACH MAVERICK

Floyd Haynes

WILDSIDE PRESS

CHAPTER ONE

When you're a boy in school ALL girls aren't appealing to you . In your classes they vary in sizes, shapes, some with black hair, others with blonde or red hair. There's usually one particular girl who tantalizes your desires during the dull moments in your class rooms.

Carol Devon didn't exactly tantalize me; rather she stood out from any other girl. For her fourteen years she was mature; slightly under five feet tall, and she weighed about one hundred pounds. She was one of those brave girls who had her hair clipped and didn't seem to worry about what anybody thought of her.

It wasn't difficult for some of the teachers to catch me looking at her as she tossed her short, red hair and straightened her bangs now and then. We had all the same classes except Home Room and Physical Education. In some class rooms it was necessary for me to glance back to see her, as in each room we sat in different areas. I'd never caught her noticing me, and I entertained no hopes that she ever would.

One sunny, May day, the lean year 1932, I met Carol on the beach, between Venice and Playa Del Rey. Her head was nearly turned and, as she walked along the beach, her eyes were staring far beyond me, like she was unaware anybody else was near.

"Hello, Carol," I said, nodding and continuing to walk.

When she looked at me she was frowning, the

way one does when glancing into the sunlight.

"Hello," she said, stopping.

My feet dug into the sand, halting me and I turned to face her.

"I don't mean to be rude," she said, "but am I supposed to know you?"

"I guess not," I said, embarrassed. "We go to the same school. I see you in all my classes."

"I know now!" she said, the frown leaving her face. "You're the kid called Allan. Really, I wouldn't have recognized you if you hadn't spoken."

"I guess it's hard for a girl to recognize every guy in school."

"That's a fact! You're pretty quiet,—maybe that's why I hadn't thought of you too much. You know, I just moved to the beach. Do you live on the beach?"

"I suppose."

"You suppose? Don't you know?"

"Well, I hang around here quite a bit. My aunt lives down the Speedway a piece. Where'd you move to?"

"Just past Washington Place."

"Oh."

"I have to go now. Some of the kids and myself are going to the dog races this afternoon. Be seeing you!"

"Goodbye."

As my uncertain steps took me forward, I glanced back at her. She was pretty from the back, and her flowered dress was tightly fitted, and the sun made her hair glisten an orange red. I stopped to face the ocean, perhaps because I wanted to watch

6

her as she put distance between us. She kept a steady gait, and I saw some boys turn and stare at her. I didn't blame them.

That Saturday afternoon I was scheduled to see a woman on Venice Pier about a job. She had indicated that I might work Friday evenings, Saturday and Sunday all day, and come on the eve of any holiday. This was promising, because the few dollars I'd make would at least allow me food money. Though I had no place to live, my stubbornness overcame any practical reason why I should leave the beach.

At the close of the previous semester another relative had left Venice but I'd chosen to stay, for the purpose of remaining in the school I liked so well. Since my relative had departed, I'd made my bed anywhere possible, sometimes a parked car, under a beach pier, or sitting on a toilet stool in some rest room. Whenever a police car stopped me at night, I always gave my aunt's address, and often they persisted in taking me home.

My aunt was a young woman and often had company. Perhaps she would've allowed me quarters with her had I insisted. But I was out of place in her apartment, and knew she did well to take care of herself.

Now, as I still watched Carol walk, her form becoming smaller with each step, I asked myself how I could include her in my meager existence, even were she to favor me. How could I tell anybody that I didn't live in a house? That I didn't really live anywhere? Only my former address stood on the school records, and I'd made doubly sure not to be absent from school, which, if I had,

7

any call to my former home would've given me a-way.

Being homeless wasn't enough to convince me that I should never have Carol. But the fact that I was very homely tended definitely to put me in my place. My age and size didn't match too well; at fifteen I was nearly six feet and weighed one-sixty. My black hair was bushy and unruly, and I had a cowlick. Daily I hoped desperately I wouldn't grow any more, and even prayed my feet wouldn't get bigger than the nine and a half shoe I already wore.

One last glance at Carol caught her turning off the beach, many blocks away. The shore line turn-ed westward, enough that I could see the stucco building where I then presumed she lived. She dis-appeared and I sighed and walked onward. For the next half mile, I listened to the breakers crashing, and daydreamed that I had Carol. I owned a car and we were driving, and she sat very close to me. It's strange what a kid can be and what he can do in a daydream.

My dream was shattered when I reached Ken's house. Blond and handsome, Ken stood outside, waiting for me.

"What took you so long?" he inquired.

I just shook my head negatively and smiled at him. He was also fifteen but a sophomore, while I was a freshman. Astrologically we were alike—both born the same month and year, with a day dif-ference in our ages. I was one day older, and oc-casionally reminded him of this fact.

"If this wasn't day time," he said, "I'd think you had stars in your eyes! What's the matter with

8

you?"

"I just saw her again—on the beach," I said.

"Saw who?"

"Carol Devon."

"I should've known! She's the only girl you ever see. Come on, let's get going. I have to get back early and help Mom with the washing."

I commenced walking and he kept pace with me. It seemed there were only a few differences between Ken and me. I liked a girl and he didn't. He was for football, and could run like a jack rabbit. I liked football but I couldn't do much of anything but tackle, if somebody ran into me. He *was* much surer of himself than I was. Otherwise we were like two bugs in a rug and liked the same activity.

"Think that woman'll let you work there?" he asked.

"I don't know. She talked like she really needed somebody. I *have* to get some kind of a job, Ken!"

"Mom raps me pretty hard across the rump a lot, but I guess I'm luckier than you are. Did you eat anything to day?"

"No," I admitted. "But I'm not hungry."

"Mom gave me a quarter for hamburgers," he said. "We can stop at the end of the pier where they have those big ones."

"You didn't tell your mother anything about me, did you?"

"No! I don't tell anybody *anything* about you. You ought to know that. She just thinks I'm a pig because of the extra sandwich I take to school."

"I'll do you a favor someday," I told him.

"You do me a favor everyday!" he said. "You're the best friend I have."

9

I guess I was, too. I thought the world of Ken. When he got hurt I felt as if I were the one who'd been injured. He smoked but I didn't. When I saw long cigarette butts, I'd always manage to pick them up for him, sometimes having to wait some endless time to avoid being seen. Nobody liked to shoot a snipe while somebody watched.

We finally reached the pier. The place I was going was about half way to the end. It was one of those places where you threw balls and knocked over wooden milk bottles, then won a prize if you knocked all of them over with a certain number of balls. My job would be to replace the bottles, something like a pin setter in a bowling alley.

I pointed to the place and Ken lingered behind. As I approached the concession, the fear in me must have been due to my lack of confidence. The woman was pleasant and heavy; very nice looking. She remembered me and immediately began explaining my duties. I was so happy I hardly heard what she said, except it was expressly understood that I'd start Sunday.

When Ken and I were some distance away he said, "I see stars in your eyes again. Did you get the job?"

"Yes," and there was a lump in my throat. "I start tomorrow."

"I'm sure glad, Allan!" and he turned, caught my hand, and began to shake it.

"Thanks, Ken."

"Let's get on out to that hamburger stand. I wonder how much that woman'll pay you?"

"I don't know. One kid I met once used to get a dollar where he worked. If I got that, and I worked three times a week, that'd be three dollars. Maybe I could get me another pair of cords for school."

"That's something funny," he said. "Almost everybody wears tan cords, but you wear black ones. Why?"

"I don't like to be just like the other guys," I said.

"I wish I was hungry," he said. "I ate so much breakfast I don't think I can eat a hamburger."

"Eat something else," I suggested, knowing full well he was planning on having me eat *two* hamburgers.

"I'm just not hungry. You could eat two hamburgers, couldn't you?" he asked.

"I guess. You could have a coke, couldn't you?" I asked.

"I don't even want a coke."

Two hamburgers and a coke for Allan. That's the way he had it figured. Think of the other guy, never about *himself*. We reached the joint and just the smell of hamburgers and onions did something to me. Gastric juices began running from my mouth into my stomach. Ken ordered for me and we stood, elbowing the outside counter.

"They smell good, don't they?" I asked him.

"Not to me! I'm too full."

The average depression kid our age could eat a hamburger for desert, but I didn't argue with him. The hamburgers came and I began eating. Ken saw a sizable snipe on the boardwalk and he began angling to get it, without being detected. Suddenly he dropped a box of matches near the butt, then, with one sweeping snatch, he scooped up both the matches and the cigarette butt.

11

Within fifteen minutes we were going back. We took the board walk until it ran out, then cut to the sand along the water.

"Let's duck under the Coast Guard Pier," Ken suggested. "If I don't have a smoke now, it'll be too fresh on my breath when I get home."

"Have you been caught lately?" I asked.

"Not since I told you about Mom catching me."

It didn't matter how many times somebody caught Ken smoking, he'd always smoke the first chance he got. I could've smoked anytime I wanted to, still the desire never came to me. It was funny to me why parents kept things from kids, or at least tried to. Ken's mother smoked, and so did his step-father.

We stopped near his house and chatted briefly. I thanked him for the hamburgers, and we made an agreement to meet late in the afternoon. Reluctantly we parted and I walked on to my beach domain, watching closely as I passed Carol's house. She wasn't in sight, and I pictured her sitting in the grand stand, watching the dog races.

From beneath the small pier where I often slept, I got my only two shirts and went to my aunt's apartment to wash and iron them. So long as I was careful I could make the school week out on two clean shirts, and once each week I washed my *cords* and *blue jeans*. If my aunt didn't intend being home on Saturdays, she'd always leave the key under the outside mat so I could get in to wash and iron my clothes. This day she wasn't home, so I took a good bath and tended to my clothes as well.

12

CHAPTER TWO

The door to Carol's life came ajar. The following Monday, in our first class, she waved to me from across the room. My pulse quickened and I experienced a new thrill. I made no attempt to stop her between classes but I did watch her closely after the bell, which dismissed our last class. Sure enough, she caught the same bus that I'd been taking and, instead of waiting for Ken, I hurried to get on behind her.

By the time Ken reached the bus all the seats were taken and he had to stand. I was two rows behind Carol, and several times she glanced back at me. To reach Washington Place it was necessary for us to transfer from the bus to a streetcar, and ride South on Pacific Avenue. Ken lingered back, waiting until both Carol and I were on the streetcar before he boarded it. Carol took a seat and moved toward the window, sweeping her skirt close to her legs. I hesitated until she smiled and glanced at the space beside her.

When Ken saw the action, he chose a seat ahead of us and, for all Carol knew, he and I were unacquainted.

"God!" Carol gestured, "I wanted to be *anywhere* but in school today. What'd you do yesterday?"

"Worked."

"On Sunday?"

"Yes."

"Where?"

"On the Amusement Pier."

13

"Venice or Ocean Park?"

"Venice Pier."

"What do you work at there?"

"You know those places where you knock over wooden bottles with baseballs?"

"Yes."

"I work in one of them. When they knock over the bottles, I set them up again."

"Well. I didn't know you worked. I saw you go by our house yesterday morning. I started to holler at you from the window."

I wish you had, I thought. I wish you'd holler at me all day long.

"Why didn't you?" I asked.

"Because Mother was there. You can stop sometime when she isn't there. She won't be home when I get there. She usually gets home about six."

I didn't know if she was inviting me or not, and I was afraid to ask. It was a certainty that Ken had heard her, but the few other people on the car likely weren't paying any attention to us. Usually I got off with Ken and walked by his house. But this time I let him get off and I rode on to Washington Place where she had to get off.

After we'd gotten off and started to walk toward Speedway she said,

"Do you like punch?"

"Yes."

"Do you want some punch?"

"I'd like some."

"Okay. You wait on the beach until I signal you from the window. Then you just walk between the houses and come in from the side. Nobody knows us yet, but somebody might snitch."

14

She was looking at me and I nodded.

"When we get to the corner, you just keep walking toward the beach, and I'll go down the Speedway. Got it?"

"Yes."

I obeyed and took my time to reach the beach. There wasn't time for me to dash to where I lived under the pier to put away my books, so I hung onto them, shifting them from one hand to the other. The breakers were nearly silent as I stood with my back to the water, waiting for her signal. Finally I saw her at the window and she was motioning for me to come.

The house was furnished beautifully and it made me feel out of place.

"Put your books on the library table and come on in the kitchen with me," she said. "We had some people over last night and there was some punch left."

Somehow, as I followed her, there was a peculiar sensation in my stomach. Both the house and Carol made me feel so small and unimportant.

"Your mother has a lot of money, hasn't she?" I managed to ask.

"I don't really know. She works, and when my father was living he had quite a bit of money. You know, he was a flier, and he was killed in his plane."

"I'm sorry!"

"So am I," she said. "Dad was a great guy. You can sit in the nook if you like."

She poured two glasses of punch and put them on the table. She sat first, then said,

"Go ahead. Sit down. You act bashful."

15

"I guess I'm sort of afraid, since I know your mother wouldn't like it if she knew I was here."

"She won't know."

I sat and picked up the glass of punch.

"Do you smoke?" she asked.

"No."

"I do. I'm going to smoke now, so all the smoke'll get out before Mother comes."

I watched her pull a single cigarette and match from one of her pockets, and figured she must've put it there after getting home from school. She put the thing in her mouth and handed me the match. I struck it and lit the cigarette. After one long drag she said,

"How old are you?"

"Fifteen."

"I'm only fourteen. I'm up with you in school though. You're big for your age. I'll bet you won't tell anybody about me smoking, will you?"

"No."

"I didn't think so," and she took another drag. "I like to smoke. You aren't very much like a kid. You know what I mean. Juvenile. A lot of those brats in school would run at the first chance, and tell everybody about me smoking."

"You wouldn't tell on anybody, either, would you?" I asked.

"I'd die first! I'm pretty grown up for my age. I never was a tattler. You don't have anywhere to live, do you?"

"Not really."

"Well, I wouldn't tell on you. If the authorities knew you didn't have a home, they'd put you in one. You know that, don't you?"

16

"I know."

"Are you going to drink your punch?"

"When you're ready to drink yours," I said.

"I'd make you something to eat if you'd eat it. You could have a sandwich with the punch."

"I'm not hungry."

"You don't say any more than you have to, do you?"

"I don't know. Don't I say enough?"

"I guess so. You aren't always talking. That's why I didn't figure you'd blab things you see me doing. That's the trouble with young guys. They tell everything they know."

"It's sort of shameful for you to know that I have no home. Guys don't like for girls to know things like that."

"Mom says if things don't get better pretty soon, a lot more people won't have homes. She said those three restaurants just closed up a while back. Two on the beach, and the other one on the corner of the Speedway and Washington Place."

"I know," I said. "One of my relatives owned the one on the corner."

"And that's why you're here without a home?"

"Yes."

"You like it here, don't you?" she asked.

"Pretty well. I want to finish school."

"Do you think you can do without a home that long?"

"I'll get somewhere to stay. I have a job now."

"You can't get a place," she objected. "Soon as you tried, somebody would put the cops on you."

She was right and that was a bridge I hadn't thought of crossing. My eyes were lowered but I

17

knew she was staring at me, dragging almost steadily now on the cigarette. To help my nervousness I sipped some of the punch.

"Is it good?" she asked.

"Yes."

"The way you say 'yes'! I guess it's the polite way of saying it. Instead of 'yeah' or 'yep'."

"If it sounds funny maybe I shouldn't say it that way."

"You be just like you are!" she scolded. "Why should you be the way other people want you to be?"

"I just don't want to sound like a freak."

"You don't. There's something very nice about you. You aren't good looking, and you're poor, but..."

Her voice died away, leaving me curious. I knew I was homely, and my poverty was obvious, but I didn't know what there was nice about me.

"Do you realize there's only four more weeks of school?"

"I know. That cigarette's going to burn your fingers."

Smiling, she got up and ran water over the butt, tore it to bits and let them fall into the disposal can. After she'd sat again she said,

"I simply die for a cigarette during classes!"

"Do you know any other girls who smoke?"

"I know several. Two or three of them smoke between classes—in the washroom. But that's not for me. If I get one tiny demerit, I don't get to go away this summer."

"Go away?" I blurted.

"Sure. I have an aunt in Rhode Island. And last summer I stayed with her until school started again.

18

I just love it there!''

A slight nausea suddenly possessed me, and I tried to look beyond summer vacation, when she'd be expected to return. To her, the thought of staying three months in Rhode Island was like a powerful stimulant. Probably freedom away from her mother, I figured.

"Why so downcast?" she asked.

"I was thinking about Rhode Island." Then I sipped more punch.

"You ought to be able to go," she said, folding her hands in delight.

"Maybe I'd better leave pretty soon," I suggested. "Your mother might come home early."

"Do you have a suit?" she asked.

"What kind of suit?"

"A bathing suit."

"Sure. I get my baths in the ocean."

"Go get it and we'll go swimming. I haven't been in since last summer."

Living on the beach as I did made swimming sound unattractive. Nevertheless I agreed to go in with her. Usually I took my baths at night when the water seemed so much warmer. But one more bath wouldn't hurt me.

Carol waited until she saw me changed and near the water, before she came out. Her suit was tight and she was chestier than I'd thought. It was something to behold to see her walking toward the water, poking her hair under the flaps of her bathing cap.

"Can you ride the breakers?" she asked.

"Yes. Can you?"

"Sure. Are you going in first?"

19

"I can."

"Will you?"

I waded waist deep into the surf, then dived into a swell that threatened to wash me ashore. Beyond the breakwater I swam with a swell until it was on the verge of breaking, after which I stiffened and rode it in.

"Wasn't that fun?" she asked.

"Great," I said. "Go ride one in."

She did as I asked and she was good. We rode a few together, then lay on the sand to dry off. I wondered how often I'd get to see her before school was out. As friendly as she was, as much as she talked and confided in me, there was something missing. I wanted to touch her. Maybe take her hand. But, because of the little encouragement she'd given me, I didn't have guts enough.

Finally the time neared six o'clock and she left me to go in. It seemed like I could've stuck thirty pounds of cotton in the empty spot she'd left in me. Doggedly I ambled down the beach until I reached the pier. After I'd squeezed under and changed into my clothes, I made my way toward Ken's house.

CHAPTER THREE

The following day Carol waved only casually at me twice during all the class changes. She managed to beat me to the bus, so I waited for Ken. When the transfer took place Carol had found a girl friend who rode to within one block of where she and I were to get off. Ken knew my desires

20

so he'd left me. At the corner where Carol started to walk I hesitated.

"Aren't you coming?" she asked.

"I don't want to make a nuisance of myself."

"You won't," she promised.

I walked with her, and we walked slowly, like neither of us knew what to say, nor had any particular place to go. When we reached Speedway she said,

"I have to give the house a good cleaning when I get home. What're you going to do?"

"I don't know. Depends on what Ken's mother wants him to do at home."

"Who's Ken?"

"My friend who was on the bus with me."

"Oh. He's cute, but he looks a lot younger than you do."

"I have the size and he has the looks," I told her.

"Mother won't be home tomorrow night," she said. "Would you like to come over for a while?"

"Yes."

"Well," and she hesitated, "Mother'll leave about seven, maybe seven-thirty. I'll open the blind facing the beach when she's gone."

"All right."

It seemed like progress, though I continually reflected that she would leave for Rhode Island in June. As I walked along the beach I wondered what her mother looked like, and I pictured her as an old, crabby woman, the kind who snapped at everybody she saw. I certainly didn't dream that she'd be so completely different than I'd imagined.

My going to see Carol the next day was the first

21

secret I'd kept from Ken. We walked down Pacific Avenue into the oil field area, climbed two or three derricks, then ducked under a pier so he could smoke. About six-thirty I made an excuse, saying that I'd go to my aunt's to wash a shirt, thus leaving him at his house.

The sky was clear and it was still very light when I saw the shade raise, the signal I waited for. Carol met me at the door, and it was like my coming had been an everyday occurrence. She was calm and unsmiling, chewing on a piece of candy. After I'd cleared the door she closed it and stood with me in the middle of the room.

"I thought we'd play Rummy," she announced. "Do you know how to play?"

"No."

"I'll teach you. It's not hard. Mother and I used to play it a lot. The only thing is, you'll have to eat something. I get nervous when I'm playing cards, and I eat. But I don't like to eat alone."

I was touchy enough to believe she was using that for an excuse to feed me, thinking I was hungry. Nevertheless I nodded assent. After she'd gotten the cards I followed her to the dining room table and sat. Before she sat she moved an ashtray and several cigarettes to the table, plus the box of candy she'd been eating from.

"Have some candy," she said, pushing the box toward me.

"Thanks," and I took a piece while she lit a cigarette.

As soon as she sat she asked,

"Did you tell your friend you were coming here tonight?"

22

"No."

"Why?"

"Because I thought it was our buisness."

"It is," she said. "I think you're going to be my most valuable friend. Want to smoke with me? I don't like to smoke alone, either."

"I'll smoke with you. But I don't inhale."

"That's all right. Here," and she handed me a cigarette. "I feel safer if you smoke."

She lit the thing for me and I dragged on it until the smoke nearly strangled me. I couldn't see why anybody liked it, but I enjoyed doing things with her.

"I'm making a bad boy out of you," she told me. "At least you're a good sport."

She put her cigarette in the ashtray and began shuffling the cards. She seemed to hypnotize me when her green eyes rested upon me.

"Playing cards isn't much fun but it's about all I know to do," she said, dealing out the cards. "When there're a lot of kids together you can do a lot of things. But the minute you do anything with them, they snitch about something."

"Were you caught doing something once?" I asked.

"Not caught, but told on," she said.

"Was your mother mean about things you did?"

"No. The reason I keep things from my mother is because I'm ashamed. If she walked in here now and found you, she wouldn't say anything. But everybody says certain things aren't right, and I'd rather my mother didn't know I did some things."

"What does your mother look like?" I asked.

"Like a woman."

23

"I mean, is she pretty?"

"I'll show you," she said, getting up. "Don't look at my hand."

"I won't."

When she returned she handed me a framed photo of a beautiful woman. I gazed almost dizzily at it, and her pretty eyes with their heavenly twinkle, seemed to gaze at me. I'd have sworn she was prettier than Carol.

"She's real young!" I blurted.

"All in the way you look at it," she replied nonchalantly. "She's seventeen years older than I am."

I continued to gaze at the picture until Carol said,

"Here, let me have it. You look like a sick cow!"

I released the photo and watched her put it face down on the table. I had no idea that the gesture had a psychological meaning.

"Did you ever go with a girl, Allan?" she asked suddenly.

I fanned my cards before I answered,

"No."

"Why not?"

"I never saw anybody I liked. And besides, I'm too young to go with girls."

"In a way it's like going with me,—your being here with me."

"I guess."

"Do you like me?"

"Yes."

She was unimpressed but she picked up her cards and quickly made a fan out of them. After a short lesson on how to play Rummy, we began dropping cards. My cigarette was burning in the ashtray but Carol picked hers up occasionally for a drag. She made a quick disposal of her cards and I was left holding the bag.

"You'll catch on," she told me. "You deal this time."

I dealt and we played and I caught on. But not once did I win, though we played until ten o'clock. I suspected that my ability as a Rummy player was dulling her evening and I said,

"You're too good for me."

"You're just not interested. I think boys would sooner do something else when they're with a girl."

I nodded, though nothing else had occured to me.

"I guess I was too wound up in skunking you to think of eating. I'll make us a sandwich."

As usual I hadn't eaten since lunch and the sandwich idea appealed to me. Aimlessly I shuffled the cards while she made sandwiches. I tried to muster some hope that Carol had reasons other than lonely ones for having me there. But lacking confidence in myself I decided it was strictly loneliness.

She brought the sandwiches. They looked so good I must have unconsciously licked my lips.

"I'll bet you're starved!" she said. "Do you like milk?"

"Yes."

"So do I. I'll get it, but you can start eating if you like."

I chose to wait for her, as I certainly didn't want her to know how really starved I was. When you figure I'd had one sandwich at noon that day,

25

and it was after ten o'clock, evidence was there. Normally I didn't care for sweet milk but whenever a glass presented itself I'd always force it down. The glass she finally placed before me was inviting.

"You need a lot of milk," she told me.

"Yes," I agreed, picking up the sandwich.

Carol didn't eat as gracefully as her usual manners would indicate. Her bites were hurriedly taken and it seemed she swallowed without thoroughly chewing her food. Thankfully enough, she paid little attention to my eating, which lessened my embarrassment a bit. To make sure I wouldn't be left eating alone I also hurried. Some milk in my glass was all that was left when she'd finished.

"We have some store cake," she announced.

When I didn't reply she asked,

"Would you like some cake?"

"I don't believe so," I said, half hating myself for it.

"Push that candy over here," she said. "I think I'll have a piece of that instead of cake."

I passed the candy and, instead of taking the box, she took one piece, leaving me hold the box.

"Keep it over there so I won't get into it so many times."

"Are we going to play cards any more?" I asked returning the candy to its place on the table.

"No. I wish there was something else to do besides play cards. Anyhow, we don't have too much time. Maybe another hour Mother'll be home. Let's smoke another cigarette. I have plenty."

"All right."

We lighted up and began filling the room with smoke. Behind a blue haze she said,

26

"I'm making a bad boy out of you! I'll bet you think I'm a little hussy."

"I don't think that."

"If you knew all the things I wanted to do, you would."

"How do you know?" I asked innocently.

"I just know you would. I'm pretty wild. But there's no fun in life the way some people live it. By the time you're old enough to have fun, it's time to get married. What fun can you have after you're married?"

"I don't know."

"Of course you don't. You've never been married. I don't think you've even kissed a girl."

"I haven't."

"Did you ever want to?"

"Sure."

"Why didn't you?"

"I didn't think the girl wanted me to."

"Who was she?"

"You."

"You're a case!" and she began laughing. "All you had to do was just kiss me! I've kissed boys before."

My total embarrassment surely popped out like the measles. Carol was still laughing, and she slapped the table with both palms. Finally she sobered and said,

"I wasn't laughing at you, Allan. But you're such a big lug! Don't you know a wild girl like me likes to be kissed? Don't you know I'm adventuruous?"

"I don't know anything about girls," I mumbled.

"I know," and she rose and began picking up

the plates. "But you can't get a girl by not knowing about them. They aren't all like they pretend to be. The reason I'm telling you this is because I know now you don't squeal everything you know or hear. You have to be forceful and demanding with a woman. I even heard Mother tell that to a man."

Since she wasn't looking at me I watched her until she went to the kitchen with the dishes. Even though she'd told me what to be like, and that it was necessary to be that way, I didn't know how to start. I was afraid. I wanted more than ever to kiss her. When she came back she stood before me.

"To kiss a girl," she commenced, "you have to first work up to it. You take my hand. Go on, take it. Now. Stand up. Okay. What do you think you should do now?"

I squeezed her hand and looked deeply into her gazing eyes. With or without experience I knew what I wanted to do. Her face was tilted and I bent slowly down to reach her lips. I didn't make a production of the gesture until both her hands flew around my neck. After my arms went around her, I guess you'd say my lips *crushed* against hers. It was so exciting that I didn't recall too vividly what actually happened.

When I felt her arms loosening I dropped mine to my sides.

"You see?" she said. "You really knew how to do it. Now, am I not a hussy?"

"No."

"I think so," she contradicted. "Showing a boy how to kiss me, and practically begging him to, isn't at all lady-like."

28

"Do you care?" I asked.

"No," and she laughed. "Not with you. But if you were a snitcher and other people found it out, and it got back to Mother, I'd care."

"It won't get back to anyone," I promised.

"Do you want to go now? I have to bathe, and Mother'll be back pretty soon anyhow."

"Yes, I'll go. Thanks, Carol, for the sandwich and milk."

"You're welcome. Good night, Allan."

"Good night, Carol!"

My departure was hurried but not abrupt. After I'd touched the sandy beach, the evening became part of the past, and my having kissed Carol was the only bright episode I could recall.

CHAPTER FOUR

Because of fate's strange way of shaping destinies, I didn't kiss Carol again for a long time. In classes she pretended almost that she didn't know me. She had a system on beating me to the bus, which resulted in her sitting with the same dead beat girl. Even after the usual transfer she sat with the girl. This left only the two blocks for us to walk together. Once, just a week away from the day school was to let out, I asked her,

"Doesn't your mother ever go out any more?"

"Once in a while," she answered evasively.

"Do you have a boy friend now?"

"Don't be silly, Allan! If your questions are because I haven't invited you to the house, don't let

29

it bother you. In case you haven't noticed, I'm down in my grades. And you know what'll happen if I don't make what I'm supposed to."

"You won't get to go to Rhode Island."

"Exactly. You're not so dumb after all."

Carol barely said goodbye that afternoon. My spirits were so low that I didn't even meet Ken. It was Friday night and I went early to the pier and waited for my boss to arrive. All during the evening, and the following two days, Carol's previous behavior affected whatever I tried to do.

Since I was essentially tempermental and stubborn, I remained aloof all the next week. When entering classes I didn't so much as glance at Carol. Instead of taking the bus I walked to the beach. I didn't go to Ken's house, but he sought and found me somewhere along the water's edge. Thursday evening he said,

"Allan, what's the beef with me? All this week I've been saving the sandwich until night, because you hide during lunch hour. You won't come to my house any more. Mom asked me yesterday about you. If you're sore at me, tell me."

"I'm not sore at you," I said.

"Then it's Carol Devon?"

"No, Ken, just let me be what I am, how I am."

"Allan, the past six months you've lived a life of hell. But you've always been the best sport I ever saw. I couldn't understand how you stayed so cheerful. Now you're like a dead man. You're my friend, Allan! What can I do to help you?"

We stood near the small pier and I put my hand on his shoulder. I hadn't wanted my feelings over

30

things unrelated to Ken to hurt him, nor affect our friendship. But I had withdrawn myself, closing any possible gate to my feelings.

"It is the girl, isn't it Allan?" he asked

"Partly, maybe," I said. "But please, Ken, don't think I'm sore at you! Look at this place. The ocean stretches from here to all the Pacific Islands. On the opposite side, clear to the other ocean, are hard times and hunger...Hell, Ken, you're all I had before Carol came along. Now, I'm used to her—counted on her as a friend..."

"All right, Allan! Don't say any more. I see what it is. I have my Mom, and you're my friend, and I have a bed to sleep in and I get to eat all I need. What do *you* have?"

"I have a damn lot, actually! I said. "Especially now that I can work at the Pier. I don't get too cold at night, and I have a place to wash my clothes."

Ken sighed and I took my hand from his shoulder.

"Like to take a walk with me?" he asked.

"Where to?"

"Just anywhere. It doesn't matter. I'd like to shoot a few snipes."

"I have some nice ones for you," I revealed. "Let me get them."

I crawled under the pier and got the snipes. Ken was calm when I emptied them into his hand.

"Let's get somewhere so I can light one," he suggested.

That brought a grim reflection of Carol. Two smokers, and I wondered if they might not be overly fond of one another if they should meet.

"We can take to the Coast Guard Pier," I said.

31

"But let's walk on the Speedway."

He nodded assent but I knew he suspected that I didn't want to walk by Carol's house on the beach. It wasn't that I didn't want to; it was stubborness and my low morale. While Ken and I walked, he tried to cheer me up by talking a lot of crud. Darkness was descending upon us and I doubt if he saw the peculiar expression on my face.

It was like that, talk and more talk, and under the big pier Ken smoked two butts. Finally we took to the beach and walked back to his house, chatting only briefly before he went in. I took my time going back to where I belonged, and when starting to pass Carol's house I saw both her and her mother through an undraped window.

I stopped and watched them. Carol sat listlessly in a chair, while her mother seemed engrossed in a lecture to her daughter. Mrs. Devon was beautiful even from that distance, and through the window she looked framed like the picture Carol had shown me. I wanted to be in that house. The warmness of it seemed to draw me magnetically, and I found it difficult to move my feet.

The next day was horrible. Everybody around me was happy that school was letting out, yet the fact alone tended to shadow me with gloom. At lunch time I was again forced to evade Ken, and the close of the school year found me walking alone up Washington Boulevard, kicking at small pebbles and bits of street debris.

On the Pier that night I worked only by the fact that the job had become second nature. The ugly, wooden bottles looked like Carol, the woman I worked for even looked like her. Finally everything

32

looked like her. By one o'clock I'd snapped out of it somewhat and I collected my money and started for my beach shelter. There was a bright moon that night and the tide was high, causing me to walk nearer to the line of houses which ran continously along the Speedway.

From at least a hundred yards away I eyed Carol's house. A large splotch of moonlight rested upon it, giving it even more dignity than it deserved. The windows were dark and I reflected that somewhere in there Carol lay asleep, perhaps dreaming about her summer in Rhode Island. My shoes continued kicking the sand and soon I was past the house. I breathed more freely until I heard a soft call behind me.

"Allan. Allan!"

There wasn't enough moon to tell me that it definitely was Carol. But the size of her silhouette and further circumstantial evidence lent strongly to the possibility.

"Wait, Allan!"

I waited until she reached me. When she did she took my hand and continued to walk, urging me along.

"I want to get farther away from the house," she told me. "I have to talk to you, Allan."

Silently I walked with her, feeling affectionate pressure from her hand as she squeezed mine. When we reached to where Washington Place ended at the Speedway she stopped and said,

"This is all right. There're no houses here. Sit with me, Allan."

Together we squatted on the sand, but she still held my hand.

33

"I'm leaving tomorrow," she said. "All week long you haven't come near me."

"No."

"Why, Allan?"

"I didn't want to cause you to miss your trip."

"I just barely made it, I think. Do you hate that I'm going?"

"I don't know. Maybe it's better if you do."

"Better for you, Allan?"

"Better for both of us."

"Will you still be here when I come back?"

"I don't know. My boss was telling me last week that the Probation Officer was asking how old I was, and all about me. She told him I was nineteen and didn't go to school. So I don't know if I'll be able to keep my job or not. She told me to tell everybody I was nineteen, except at school."

"You look nineteen, Allan. But if you should leave, how would I ever know where you went?"

"Why does it matter?"

"I don't know," and she rubbed one side of her face like she was trying to figure it out. "Today, when you refused again to look at me, and you weren't on the bus, I didn't know what to do."

"Carol," I said, "When we first talked I had hopes you liked me. But after you talked the way you did last week, I saw that your friendship with me was only because you were lonely."

"Of course! For what other reason do people have friends? If somebody isn't lonely, what business does she have with boy friends?"

"None, I suppose."

"Will you promise to be around when I come back?"

"How can I promise?"

"Will you try to be?"

"I don't know."

"Why won't you promise? Don't you like me the way you did when you wanted to kiss me?"

"I guess I do."

"You're a strange guy! Sometimes I think you don't know what you're living for."

"I don't really know that," I admitted.

"Look, Allan, don't fight and argue with me. If Mother should wake up and fihd me gone, it'd mean my trip is off. You see what a chance I'm taking to talk to you?"

"Yes."

"Then promise me you'll be here when I come back!"

"I can't. And if you're that worried, why're you leaving?"

"I have to leave! I've planned on it. If I told Mother now that I didn't want to go, it'd make her suspicious. And besides, she has plans for the summer, without me."

"Carol, I'll try to be here when you come back. But I don't know if I can beat out three more years as a beach comber. Maybe I'll have to quit school—not even go next year."

"I know!" she said. "If you have to leave, come back when school starts."

"What if I'm thousands of miles away?"

"You can't go that far. How would you go?"

"The same way I've lived on the beach. I'd starve and hitch hike."

"You're making this terribly hard for me, Allan. I'm having to beg you, and really I shouldn't do that! Look, Mother's marrying a very rich man pretty soon. Maybe while I'm in Rhode Island. Things might even be different when I come back, if she gets married. She won't have as much time to worry about what I might do."

"I can't promise you, Carol."

"All right. You might be sorry. I'm going to go back home now," and she rose. "I won't be able to see you again, Allan."

I got up.

"I guess if I don't see you ever again, it'll be because we're not supposed to see each other again," she said.

"I suppose."

"*Yes. No. I guess so. I suppose.* Why can't you say other things? Why can't you talk longer and say more?"

I refused to answer. I felt she was finding fault again.

"Goodbye, Allan!"

"Goodbye, Carol."

She began running like she was afraid. Slowly I walked over her tracks, to make certain that she got into her house safely. She didn't know that I followed her in such a manner because she never looked back. And neither of us knew what lay in store for us, or that it would be years before we would meet again.

CHAPTER FIVE

In July, approximately three weeks after Carol had gone, an unusual incident occurred. It was

Saturday and, as I walked along the beach, I noticed several swimming parties. One group was near Carol's house, and two of the group were laughing loudly as they watched somebody swimming beyond the surf.

"You have to give her credit!" a man said loudly.

It was then that I looked toward the sea and saw the woman. Her arms appeared nearly limp and I'd have sworn she was fighting for her life. She reminded me of another person I'd seen drown, while onlookers thought she was clowning in the water. My experience while living on the beach told me it was chancy to ignore this scene. Hurriedly I slipped off my shoes and removed my shirt, then plunged into the surf.

After jack knifing into a large swell I came to the surface and saw the woman again. This time I knew she was in trouble. I didn't panic but I swam as fast as I could. When I reached her she was out of breath and her face was in the water. After approaching her from behind, I caught her chin and yanked her head up. I kept my distance and began floating her, pulling slowly shoreward.

Fortunately the surf wasn't rough that day. We were lucky to catch a good swell, and I hugged her to me and stroked as rapidly as possible with my free hand. When the undertow commenced we were far enough in for me to stand in the surf. By then, two of the men were meeting us, and one of them took the woman from me.

I recognized fright on all their faces, and people from other swimming groups gathered around. The woman was still in fair shape but she began spitting

37

out salt water.

"I had no idea..." one of the women gestured.

"Why didn't she call?" another one said.

Fools, I thought. Plain, damn fools!

"Helen!" the man said. "Are you all right, Helen?"

She opened her eyes wider and struggled to stand. My pulse quickened when I recognized her. She was Carol's mother! For a moment our eyes met, and she was almost ghostly white, her hand against her throat. One of the women moved between us, cutting off her view of me. I turned slowly and walked to where I'd dropped my shoes and shirt, picked them up, them sauntered on down the beach.

About a quarter of a mile away I slipped off my socks and squeezed some of the water from them, after which I beat them against my hand to shake out some of the sand. My pants were a mess and I doubted if they would dry in time for me to go to work. I didn't care. I kept recalling Helen Devon's body in my arms, and seeing her white face and dripping hair. I was fully aware of the fact that I hadn't come along any too soon.

I was still pretty wet when I reached the concession. My boss looked me over but she made no comment. In my usual quiet way I took my place and waited for customers to come along to knock over the bottles....

When I returned to my nest under the pier I heard voices. My hesitation was short lived, as somehow I knew the cops were coming my way. I went hurriedly to the water and waded into the surf until I was neck deep. While I held onto a pier pile I listened to the cops talk as they searched under the pier.

"Leave everything as it is," one of the cops said. "He'll be back."

The night was light enough so that I could see them as they left the beach. I cautiously made my way back, snatched my belongings and fled Southward down the beach. The only other place I knew to camp was under the Coast Guard Pier, in the opposite direction. That was risky because the surrounding area was more heavily populated. Finally I cut back and crossed Pacific and took to the canal bank.

Not too far down I spotted a garage which belonged to an empty house. After going inside and examining its dirt floor and inhaling a goodly amount of dust, I changed my clothes and ditched the wet duds over a rafter. The beach sand never seemed like dirt to me, but that garage floor was dirt, and sleeping there didn't appeal to me.

For several hours I played cat and mouse with the police car. The cops cruised down Pacific, then Speedway, and back to Pacific again. Not very far from the pier there was a car parked, and it had been there for months, the salt air eating away at its metal and chrome. Once I tried to make it to the car but the patrol car circled the block near it. Time was running out and soon it would be daylight. After ducking between beach houses for half an hour, I finally squatted near an outside staircase, sleepy as hell.

From my position I could see if a car went down Speedway. For quite some time the coast, was clear, and I figured the cops had given up. I went around the house and lay on the sand, not realizing it was Carol's house. My eyes made half a dozen swipes at the star studded sky, then I fell asleep.

I dreamed of Helen Devon, only the situation had been reversed. She was dragging me from the water, and when we rode through the surf she was holding me closely to her. She had laid me upon the sand and the sun was drying me out. Finally, when the glare of the sun became too harsh on my eyes, I opened them. Instantly I realized that I'd dreamed and in reality I was openly lying on the beach.

Somebody was sitting beside me, a woman, and she was clad in a red dress. I rose, startled to find her so near to me.

"I was waiting for you to wake up," she said.

It was Helen Devon and I was very embarrassed.

"You must've had a hard night sleeping here," she said. "I didn't see you until about ten minutes ago."

"I haven't been here long," I told her. "I worked late, and I didn't feel like going to bed."

"I see," she said, gazing deeply into my eyes. "You know that I recognize you?"

"I recognize you too," I said. "But I wasn't here because of that."

"I know. But I wish you hadn't left so soon yesterday. I was still too frightened to thank you."

"You don't have to thank me."

"I must," she said. "I'm Mrs. Devon. And I live there," and she pointed to the house. "I owe my life to you, and I can't take it so lightly. What's your name?"

"West."

"Your first name?"

40

"Allan."

"Good. You can call me Helen. Will you come in for breakfast with me?"

"No, thanks anyhow. But I have to do some things."

"What do you have to do, Allan?"

"Well," and my hesitation brought a grin to her face.

"That's what I thought! You're shy."

She got up and reached down and took my hand.

"Come on, Allan! In the house for breakfast. I'm going to be your best friend for the rest of my life."

Goose bumps traveled over my body and her hand felt like something heavenly. Half-heartedly I followed, feeling some guilt for having previously been in her house. We reached the door and she said,

"My daughter went to Rhode Island a few weeks ago. She's fourteen. How old are you, about twenty?"

"Nineteen," I lied before thinking.

"I didn't miss it far. I'm sure glad you can swim!"

She let go of my hand and opened her door. It didn't seem like I'd been in the house before, perhaps because Carol wasn't there. I felt better, however, maybe because permission to enter had come from the highest in command. She waited until I was in, then closed the door.

"Sit down, Allan. Do you drink coffee?"

I didn't want to appear juvenile so I said,

"Yes."

"Fine. I'll get you a cup to drink while I fix breakfast. Cream and sugar?"

41

"Yes."

She smiled and I did likewise. For the first time since pulling her out of the water I valued my part in the incident. Mostly, perhaps, because I was so glad she hadn't drowned. An unpleasant chill went through me when I visualized her lying dead. How horrible that would've been, I thought.

Within ten minutes after getting the coffee she announced breakfast. We began eating in the nook and I marveled at how coincidental it was that I had returned to the house under such odd circumstances. We were having eggs and bacon, something I'd missed for many months, and I found that coffee tasted good.

"You're the quietest boy I've ever met," she told me.

"I don't mean to be. This is a nice breakfast."

"Thank you," and she picked up her napkin to touch her lips. "My friends were very upset yesterday after they learned I was drowning when you came along. I'd tried to call to them but I couldn't manage it. How did you know?"

"I saw somebody drown like that once," I said. "Everybody thought the guy was acting a fool. By the time anybody knew different, he went down."

"How horrible!"

"That was what I was afraid of when I saw you in the water."

"Thank God! I was supposed to go somewhere today with my friends but I declined. I was hoping you'd come by again."

She was looking at me but I kept eating, looking down at my plate. It was comforting when she resumed her eating, though I was nearly finished. We both were silent long enough to complete break-

42

fast, then she said,

"Where do you live?"

I'd told her one lie but I didn't want to tell another one. Without too long a wait I admitted,

"I don't live any particular place now. I was sleeping under a pier until last night, but the cops raided it."

"Sleeping under a pier?"

"Yes. I've been sort of getting by on the beach for about seven months now."

"How on earth do you live?"

"How do you mean?"

"How do you eat?"

"I work some."

"Why, you certainly aren't going to sleep under a pier any more!"

"Not that one, anyhow," I said, laughing. "Somebody must've told the cops."

"From now on," she said, "you'll live right here. The idea of your having to sleep under a pier!"

"A lot of people don't have a pier to sleep under," I told her. "And it isn't as warm every place as it is in California."

"That might be so. But so long as I have a place for you, you don't have to sleep under anything but covers."

She got up and filled our cups. I wondered what Carol would think if she'd heard that. What would she further think if she knew I'd saved her mother's life? How would she react, especially since she'd practically yanked her mother's picture from my grasp. Helen sat again and passed me the cream and sugar, after which she rose and left the room. She came back with a package of cigarettes.

"Do you smoke?" she asked, taking her seat

43

again.

"Not very often."

"Care to smoke with me?"

"I guess. I'm not in the habit yet."

She extended the pack and I took one, and she did the lighting honors.

"I guess smoking's all right, but if you aren't in the habit, you're better off without it. My daughter smokes, and I suppose she'd die if she knew I'm aware of it. I've never told her not to smoke."

I wondered if Ken's mother knew also that he smoked. Funny how parents knew about so many things kids did. And how so many kids knew so much of what their parents did under cover.

"You'd like my daughter," she told me. "She's a little devil, but she respects me enough not to be too open with what she does. I wish she would come out with it, but she won't."

What a surprise you'd get if you knew how much I already like your daughter, I thought. And I like you too, Helen Devon. You're beautiful, warm and friendly, and I'll bet you have a heart of gold!

Our eyes met and she smiled, like she'd read my mind. After inhaling a drag of her cigarette she said,

"You'll see what I mean when she comes back this fall. I hold that summer trip over her head all during school year. And I make it clear to her that if her grades are bad she doesn't get to go."

Fall? I thought. Does she expect me to stay until fall?

"I presume you finished high school?" Helen asked.

"No. I went through the ninth," and I nearly began to cough from puffing on my cigarette.

44

"Where do you work?"

"On the Amusement Pier."

"When? What hours?"

"I work Friday nights; and Saturday and Sunday. I start today at one o'clock."

"That's too bad," she said. "How late?"

"Usually till one in the morning. It depends on how busy we are. If there's not much doing, she closes early."

"I keep the house locked, so you remind me to give you a key. You can sleep in Carol's room until she gets back, then we'll plan something else."

"I can't stay here, Mrs. Devon," I objected.

"Why not," and she leaned forward to stare at me.

"It wouldn't be right to impose on you. And besides, somebody might talk."

She leaned back and pondered my statement. She took a deep drag from the cigarette, exhaled, then said,

"It wouldn't be an imposition, Allan. And what would there be for people to talk about?"

"You know how people are." I started to mention the fact that she'd just moved there but held my tongue. "I'm a pretty big kid, and somebody might think something funny about me staying here."

"Let me worry about that," she said. "If somebody thinks I'm sleeping with you, let them think it. I know my fiance won't think like that. After what happened yesterday, he'll more than likely be glad if you're around. He's out of town a lot."

"Was that him with you yesterday? The guy who took you from me?"

"Yes, it was. He felt terrible because you didn't wait."

Since there was nothing worthwhile for me to

say, I let her continue talking. She went into things about herself, such as some of her habits, and also likes and dislikes. She told me that she was fond of indulging in drinking, but she always lost her memory after so many drinks. After she'd awoke the following day with a clean slate, no recollection of what had taken place the night before.

It was noon when I left, which allowed me an hour to get to my job. I'd promised her that I'd return and spend the night. As I walked over the sand, I knew several reasons why I thought my staying in her house was a bad arrangement. One was that my motherless years had left me wanting somebody like her, yet, even at my age, I recognized a physical attraction building up in me.

CHAPTER SIX

After finishing work and trudging back to Helen's house, I used the key and entered. A suppressed light shone dimly in the dining room but she wasn't in sight. When I came into Carol's room the light was on, and the bed covers were turned back. This was like a second invitation to stay, far more emphatic than her oral plea had been.

Once in bed, with the light out, I found myself thinking both of Carol and Helen. I was confused, and the women appeared to stand apart. As dumb as I was, I knew Carol wouldn't like my being there in her absence, alone with her mother. And I asked myself what impact it would have were I to tell Helen that I had been invited to her house by her daughter.

46

The soft bed took its toll and I went off to sleep. It was semi-sleep at first, when you're neither a-wake nor asleep. But I was to recall the next day that I remembered only certain things, which indicated an early and sound sleep.

Helen was gone when I arose. Though she'd left a note instructing me to eat, I declined. I made use of the plumbing facilities, then straightened up the bed in which I'd slept. My next move was to heat the coffee and, after sugaring up a cup, I took a chair near the window which faced the beach. For the longest time my gaze swept over the ocean surf.

I'll never know what I saw that morning, or what it was that turned my mind against the beach surroundings. Maybe it was fear that one day I would no longer be able to survive there, or perhaps hatred for what had occurred in the past. Nevertheless I grew restless, and any future I might have previously seen for myself was dimmed to nothingness.

It was gratifying when I saw Ken, clad in swimming trunks, walking along the beach. Evidently he was heading for the pier to search for me. Quickly I raised the window and called to him. A peculiar look crossed his face as he stared at me.

"Come on up!" I called.

"Who's there?" he wanted to know.

"Just me!"

Lazily he climbed the slight incline and came to the door. He stood there gazing around, as if he suspected that I'd lied to him. Finally he stepped inside and I closed the door.

"How come?" he asked, looking over the house.

"How come what?"

"How come you're in here?"

47

"I live here."

"I thought she left town."

"Carol did, but her mother's still here. Come over and sit down. You can smoke. Do you have a butt?"

"You won't believe it but. . ." and he pulled out a package of cigarettes.

"High-toned!" I remarked. "Sit down, Ken. It's all right."

"Not any higher-toned than this house you're living in."

We sat but he continued to look strangely at me. He wanted an explanation, something I wasn't going to give him. I couldn't see telling him about the ocean rescue of Helen Devon. He lit a cigarette, then hung one leg over the chair arm.

"This is class," he remarked. "Maybe I ought to get me a girl friend."

"The cops were looking for me night before last," I told him.

"No fooling! Is that why you're here?"

"Yes," which was partly true.

"Did that probation officer come back any more?"

"No. But I've been telling everybody I'm nineteen."

"What about when you go back to school?"

"I've thought of that, Ken. I don't think I can make school next year. Just before you came by I was thinking of leaving the beach."

"I hope not," he said. "Maybe you could work out something and stay here —in this house."

"No. But there's a few more weeks to think about it."

Anything else we discussed wasn't worth mentioning. At noon we struck out toward the Amusement Pier, ending up at the hamburger joint. I told Ken

48

a little fib about having promised Helen to help her that evening, thus setting things up for an early parting. Something about Helen made me enjoy her, and I wanted to be there when she got home.

Helen was home a few minutes before I got there and, when I went in, she acted happy to see me, like maybe she suspected that I'd never come back. That was gratifying and I was pleased with the situation. She had planned cold cuts for dinner and had begun preparing salad. Relaxed and smiling, I took a seat in the nook.

"It would've been lonesome here without you," she said. "Last summer when Carol went away, we lived inland. When I was completely alone I ate most of my meals out."

"This is the worst time of the day to be alone," I told her. "Every day at this time I feel terrible."

She stopped, thought for nearly a minute, then said,

"It's funny you'd say that. That's how I feel! Sometimes I get morbid when the sun sets."

"How often does your boy friend come?"

"He comes Friday and usually leaves Sunday. You know, Allan, he's a strange sort. Sometimes I wonder if I'm the only woman he goes with."

She went on messing with the salad, and I watched her closer than ever. I recalled the guy's face, and I didn't care much for him. I'd been told many times, however, that kids were prone to dislike people for no reason at all, and for the world I wouldn't have told Helen how I felt.

"He's younger than I am," she pursued. "Maybe that doesn't matter."

"I've heard people say it doesn't," I offered.

"His family is quite well-to-do," she said "He's

out here, trying to prove himself to his family.''

''If he does that, then they'll give him some of the money?'' She laughed and said,

''Probably. I'll bet you have girl friends, don't you?''

''No.''

''None at all?'' and she turned to stare at me.

''None at all.''

''Bet you don't like girls.''

''I like them all right. But I don't like all of them. You know how I mean. I wouldn't want to kiss all of them.''

This was amusing to her and she went overboard with laughter. It didn't embarrass me, just like being there with her didn't. She was just that kind of person, or at least she affected me that way.

''You're certainly a fine looking boy,'' she said.

Her compliment should've given me confidence. It didn't, but at the same time I believed that she saw me just as she stated. Had anybody else told me that, I'd have been offended and would've considered it a lousy joke.

I guess you'd say I took to Helen like a duck takes to water! All during dinner we laughed and talked, and afterwards we sat in the front room and talked a lot more. She told me things about herself that she'd doubtless told others. She even told me how passionate she was, and how she tried constantly to control herself. She'd had no sexual relations with Jim Darwin, her fiance, and didn't intend to have unless they married. She said that in the beginning of their romance he'd slipped up by indicating that a woman who would have premarital relations with a man wasn't much good.

"Then," she told me, "he gripes now and then because I *won't give in to him.* My God, Allan! What does he expect?"

I shook my head, like it was a shame for him to have been stupid. And it was easy to see that she would've been a fool to let him have her, after he'd voiced such an attitude.

"You know what I'd like to have, Allan?"

"What?"

"A little drink. Would you like one?"

"I've never had one. But I'll try it once."

"I hope you don't think I'm trying to lead you astray."

"I won't think that. What's wrong with it?"

"Nothing, except I could be put in jail for giving it to you."

"I know where I can get whiskey if I want it. I know some kids who get it all the time. The reason I've never wanted it, I guess, is because I could get it if I wanted to."

"Maybe that's why Carol never touched whiskey. It's always here, but she's never taken any. I don't leave cigarettes here, yet she smokes. She buys them out of her allowance."

"I don't think having a drink with you will make a drunkard out of me."

"Right! I'll mix us some cokes."

Helen must've made my drinks weak, for all I tasted was a new sharpness as compared to an average coke. Hers, however, were no doubt much stronger, because a change came over her after five drinks. I could feel some difference in myself, too, but it was only an exhilarating sensation.

Suddenly she turned on the radio. Back she came, dancing over the thick rug.

51

"Let's dance!" she said, reaching for my hands.

"I don't know how," but I was already up and she was in my arms.

"I'll teach you. Listen to the music and I'll lead you."

I was clumsy but I tried. Though I stepped on her feet many times, she was patient.

"You're getting it!" she exclaimed. "That's it! Keep it up."

The station threw in a commercial. We disengaged ourselves to go back to our cokes.

"That was fun," she said. "I love to dance. Jim doesn't dance and he won't let me teach him. It wouldn't take you any time at all to learn."

"Do you want to know something, Mrs. Devon?"

"Yes, Allan."

"I certainly do like you!"

"Bless you!" and she moved to the arm of my chair and ran her fingers through my hair. "I like you an awfully lot, too."

"It was all right for me to tell you, wasn't it?" I asked.

"Of course it was. And you call me Helen, will you?"

"Yes. I like these cokes."

"So do I," and she moved back to her chair. "I feel real good. and I could just dance and dance——— and maybe float away into the air!"

I was ashamed for the way I felt about her. She was trying to be nice to me and, ungrateful as it would appear, I'd become physically aroused, afraid to get up from the chair for fear she'd see. When another song started to play I suggested,

"Let's wait and try the next one."

"Good," she said. "I'll spike our glasses a-

52

gain."

Helen was persistent, and she kept me trying to dance. It appeared that the more she danced the gayer she felt, and she kissed me several times on my cheeks. She constantly admonished me for being too stiff, not relaxing while I danced. I had to be that way, making sure our bodies didn't touch at the wrong time. For the world I wouldn't have unnecessarily revealed any physical attraction for her.

Our party lasted until eleven o'clock. Like a devoted mother she turned back the covers of my bed and fluffed the pillows, and turned on the bed lamp. When she returned to the front room she relaxed in a chair and sighed.

"Tonight was fun!" she said.

"Yes," I managed to say. "It was the most fun I guess I ever had."

"You're so appreciative, Allan! You remind me so much of my late husband. He was a big brute but kind as they came. You know, I can't recall that he ever frowned. And I've never seen you frown yet."

"I think people frown a lot because of the sun."

"I don't mean that kind of frowning," she said. "I'm talking about the grouchy kind."

"I see."

"Well, we'd better put us to bed. I have a big day tomorrow. I manage a clothing store, and we have to get a big sale under way."

I got up and she turned out a few lights. When I was sure she was headed for her bedroom I said,

"Goodnight, Helen."

"Nighty-night!"

CHAPTER SEVEN

The following weekend I met Jim Darwin. He was a handsome man, twenty-seven years old, and he was as blond as I was brunette. He was slightly shorter than I but weighed more. He was the type of guy who stopped at every mirror to check his appearance, reassuring himself that both his hair and necktie were in place.

I didn't meet him until after work Friday night. He and Helen had been out somewhere and had come home only a short time before I'd arrived. I tried to get to my room immediately after the introduction but Helen wouldn't allow it.

She mixed a drink for me and, while I listened to them talk, I sipped it, noticing that Jim kept an occasional eye in my direction. After a while he turned completely toward me and said,

"I'm certainly grateful to you, Allan, for staying around to look out for Helen while I'm away."

"Thanks," I said.

"I guess you boys know," Helen remarked, "that I've stopped swimming for a while."

"You won't have any problem while Allan's around," Jim said, I hurried with the drink, then excused myself. This time it worked, and I managed to get to my room. It was possible that Helen believed Jim liked the idea of my being around. But for a certainty, I *knew* he didn't. Sleep was late in coming, and about two-thirty I heard Jim leave. That was a relief and I felt I could go to sleep, and would have, had Helen not knocked on my door.

"Sleep, Allan?"

"No, Helen."

I switched on the bed lamp as the door opened.

54

She came in and sat on the edge of the bed.

"What do you think of Jim?" she asked.

"Seems like a great guy," I said.

"I don't know," she said. "He acted strangely tonight."

"All evening. Something else. He told me he was going back to New York, and wouldn't be here again for three weeks."

"Is that strange?"

"Unusual," she said. "Honestly, Allan, I wouldn't have thought anything at all about it — were it not for the peculiar way he acted tonight."

"Something on his mind, that's all. Tomorrow, everything'll be all right."

"Perhaps," and she rose. "What time do you want to get up in the morning?"

"I'm going to work at noon. But I'd like to get up at least when you do. "

"I'll call you. Thanks for the encouragement!"

Her goodnight was almost inaudible and I knew she was unhappy. I began to recall the week I'd been there, and the wonderful evenings we'd spent together. It had been more fun than I ever hoped to have with anybody else, especially under such circumstances. She had given me confidence that one day somebody would want me, and she'd voiced her own need for my friendship. All of this was reason enough for my not wanting to see her unhappy.

The next morning we had breakfast together, after ten o'clock. The atmosphere was heavy, and Helen's brow was knitted. I'd heard remarks about women being unpredictable and it seemed best for me to remain quiet. Of course at that time I had no idea that she was suspicious of any particular thing concerning Jim Darwin, I might have compared her problem with my own, when I'd suspected that her daughter didn't care to have me around.

"I wish you weren't working today," she said. "Somehow I feel I need you."

I pondered her wish, and at the same time sought a solution. As always, when in trouble, you think of your friends. My thoughts reached out for Ken. He'd be the very one to help me, so I could help Helen.

"I'll go see if my friend will take my place," I told her.

"You might lose your job," she said.

"I don't know. I don't really care."

"No, Allan. It's not that necessary."

"I'll be back after a while," I said.

She didn't object. I broke out of the house and beat it for Ken's place. In my juvenile mind the situation was a crisis, and my child-like gallantry was pushing to the surface.

Along with being surprised to see me, Ken was pleasantly receptive to my proposal. After a brief conference with his mother, he reported that the deal was cinched. I gave him a few last minute hints, then went back to Helen.

Helen's concern was split between my losing my job and her losing her beau.

"It's probably only a silly idea," she warned me. "I wish I hadn't let Carol go up there."

"What's that?" I asked.

"Carol," she said. "I might as well tell you, Carol has a child infatuation for Jim. But surely Jim wouldn't go up there and try to be with her!"

That shook me plenty. Carol, fourteen, Jim twenty-seven. It could be possible. What about

56

Helen's being thirty-one, and Jim's being twenty-seven?

"How do you know that about Carol?" I asked.

"It's easy to know," she said. "The problem is what to do about it. With Carol it'll blow over. But what if Jim tries to take advantage of it? From the way he acted yesterday..."

"I don't think so," I said. "I think you're worrying over nothing. He's a good-looking guy, and I'll bet he can get all the girls he wants, his age and older-or even younger."

I got her attention and realized immediately I'd opened my mouth as the hook passed by.

"That's so, Allan. Only I've tried to hide from it. As I get older, Jim will want his women younger."

"Why, you could get men by the carloads!" I said. "You could get all you wanted, even younger than he!"

She smiled vaguely and sighed, like she thought I was the prize of all jokers. I didn't understand her type of fear then. Nor did I understand why she'd actually been going with Jim. You don't really try to fathom things until they concern you.

"Jim's plenty young," she agreed, "and I don't know how I could manage anyone younger."

"Well, I don't think any girl, no matter how young, can beat your time with Jim."

"Men like to play," she said. "Sometimes with young things."

As soon as her statement soaked in, I imagined I saw Jim playing with Carol; he was playing with everything, touching her all over, and Carol was giggling with delight. It wasn't such a joke because I liked Carol, and suddenly I became silently enraged with jealousy.

"I'll fool him!" Helen said, snapping me back to reality.

"Little Miss Carol will just get her butt back here. Whether or not I'm wrong, I think she's safer here anyhow."

"I can't seem to believe that," I told her, trying to convince myself that Carol wouldn't let Jim take liberties with her. "Let's do the dishes, and I'll bet Jim comes after a while, and everything'll be fine."

"That's why I needed you!" she said. "You're the most optimistic person I've ever met. Let's see what happens."

We did the dishes. She washed and I dried. As minutes passed, I seethed with boiling emotion as regards Carol and Jim. Carol had warned me that she was wild. She'd proved to me that she at least liked to be kissed. Optimistic. Helen said I was optimistic. She wouldn't have thought so had she read my mind. She was wiping the drain board when her doorbell rang.

"Get out of the kitchen, Allan," she said. "I don't want him to see you helping."

I walked behind her, then passed her when she stopped at the door. I lounged lazily in a chair.

"Hello, Ruby!" Helen exclaimed. "Come on in."

"I took a chance," the girl said. "Didn't know if you'd be here or not."

Ruby cast her eyes on me the second she was inside. Helen glanced at me, then back at Ruby.

"Meet Allan West, Ruby."

I rose, and nodded.

"Hello, Allan. Isn't he the boy...?" And she looked at Helen.

"He's the one," Helen said. "Sit down, Ruby."

58

She took a chair opposite me and smiled broadly at me when I sat down. She was an oval-faced brunette, with dark eyes and long lashes. She wore a lavender dress trimmed in white lace, and her hair was quite long but curled neatly. She was taller than Carol, heavier, but not quite as bosomy.

Helen fired a cigarette and sat down. I didn't know what to do with my hands, and I became very nervous because of Ruby's close scrutiny. I couldn't tell her age. She looked young, in her late teens or early twenties. It was obvious that she was curious about my being in Helen's house.

"Do you and Jim have any special plans for tonight?" Ruby asked.

"Not yet," Helen said. "I don't know what time he's coming by."

"I had a date with Perry for tonight, but it turns out he has to work."

"Oh?" and Helen frowned sorrowfully.

Ruby looked at me again, catching me staring at her. She smiled and I reciprocated with a grin. She turned slightly and looked at Helen.

"Do you like it any better here?" she asked.

"I believe so," Helen said. "I'm getting used to hearing the breakers roar. I like your dress, Ruby."

"Thank you. I splurged yesterday, and I thought Dad would die when he saw the bill!"

"Doesn't he always fuss?" Helen asked, laughing. "He probably blames me, thinks I lure you into the store. We're getting something in next week you'd like."

"Not yet," she said. "Wait till Dad gets over yesterday."

As they changed the subject I began to catch

the warmness in Ruby's voice, and the depth of her mind. I gathered from their discussion that she was near twenty. She stated that she definitely wasn't going to college, as she figured her place was in a home, being a house-wife. Finally, when Helen left us to make coffee, Ruby asked,

"How old are you, Allan?"

"Nineteen."

"Oh."

She shifted her position and pulled the skirt of her dress over her knees.

"You ought to get a job being a life guard," she said.

"You have to be twenty-one for that," I informed her.

"It seems to me like everybody has to be twenty-one for anything," she said. "That's all I hear from my dad. He says wait till I'm twenty-one."

I nodded, smiling politely. It was easy to see that Ruby was ready to unleash a gust of dissatisfaction with life. Fortunately, Helen came back, and Ruby turned her conversation toward another topic. During those moments I hoped Ruby would leave soon, so Helen and I could be alone.

Luck wasn't in my favor that day. Ruby stayed on and on. We finished a pot of coffee, went through half a hundred records from Helen's albums, and both Ruby and Helen taught me some dance steps. As the afternoon raced nearer to night, Helen brought out the hard drinks.

CHAPTER EIGHT

Jim Darwin showed up about seven. Spread before us were sandwiches and empty coke bottles, remains of a feast we'd had earlier. The disgusted look on Jim's face was obvious to us all.

"Started early," he said, caustically.

"Sure," Ruby piped up. "Why didn't you come along before now?"

"Busy," he mumbled.

"Find a chair and make yourself at home, Jim," Helen said. "I'll fix you a drink."

"Never mind," he said. "I don't want a drink. We were scheduled to meet some friends tonight."

"I didn't know, Jim," Helen said. "Why didn't you tell me? The phone hasn't rung all day."

"Can you get ready?" he asked, still standing.

"I can. Won't you have a drink?"

"No."

"Ruby," and Helen hesitated, "Would you and Allan excuse me for the balance of the evening?"

"Of course! Maybe he and I'll take a Saturday night walk. How about that, Allan?"

"Fine, I guess."

Smiling broadly, Helen rushed to her bedroom to get ready. Jim paced the floor, and occasionally Ruby winked at me. I was uncomfortable, and I disliked Jim more than ever. It was pretty clear that, either he had plans which precluded Helen, or he was jealous. I hadn't forgotten the seed Helen had planted in my mind; that he likely wanted to play with Carol.

Jim left without saying anything at all to Ruby and me. While Helen bid us goodnight, he waited outside. As soon as we heard the car roar away, Ruby said,

"He's got a hell of a nerve! Imagine! He was mad because she wasn't sitting here by herself,

61

waiting for him!"

"Maybe he had a flat tire," I suggested.

"He's flat himself," she said. "I think he *knew* Helen was drowning,—that day you pulled her out of the water."

"Really?"

"Sure. And he *dared* her to swim out there. I'd just told him he ought to go after her—not a minute before you came along."

I figured Ruby was being slightly dramatic, and that she was letting her dislike for Jim get the best of her. She was pretty wobbly from the cokes and whiskey she'd had, and she'd become careless about her dress creeping too high above her knees.

"I guess you're stuck with me for the rest of the evening, Allan," she said. "I'll bet you like Helen awfully well, don't you?"

"Yes."

"In a way, you know, she's yours."

"What's that?"

"Helen's really *yours*," she said. "You saved her life, and if you hadn't, she wouldn't be here."

"That doesn't mean she's mine," I objected.

"Maybe not. But she likes you, and you like her."

"I like you too, Ruby," I told her.

She laughed, cutting her eyes sharply at me.

"Now, now, Allan! I think this bootleg whiskey's getting you. You don't even know me! Besides, I'm a spoiled brat."

"Why?"

"Because I get everything I want. My daddy spoils me rotten."

"How did you happen to know Helen?" I asked.

"She used to live next door to us until she moved over here. Have you met Carol?"

62

"No. She'd left for Rhode Island before I met Helen."

"She's a real spitfire. And she'll cuss a blue streak if she gets mad at you. You ought to see her go ga-ga when she's around Jim! Boy!"

When I remained silent she said,

"I guess you aren't interested in things like that. Let's drink some more, then dance. I feel real reckless!"

I remained neutral to her proposal. Satan was dancing in her black eyes but I was too inexperienced to know the sign. She poured whiskey unsparingly into glasses, then slopped in some coke. The first sip I took burned my stomach, but she drank hers without a frown.

Several times I caught a glimpse of what she normally might have kept concealed, that part of her body which the average boy watches for. The lack of modesty was strickly carelessness, for which reason, I suppose, I wasn't moved. Her lingerie was pink, and the panties were lace-trimmed.

After she'd drank the potent glass of fire, she began weaving in the chair. It had taken only one strong shot to finish the job.

"Let's go for a walk," I suggested, watching her rub her temple, knowing she was trying to figure what had hit her.

"One more drink!" she said, throwing back her head. "I'm reckless. If I get in the water, pull me out, Allan boy!"

I wasn't smart enough to take her outside, whether or not she agreed. But I did refuse to give her my glass for another spiking, though she mixed another strong one for herself.

63

"You want to know why I feel reckless?" she asked, waving the glass at me.

"I'd like to know," I said.

"Because nobody wants me! That's why. Do you think my daddy wants me? No! He tells me to go find myself some fun. See, Allan? I'm finding myself some fun."

"Yes."

"I ought to be married," she said. "But nobody wants me. You want to know the truth about tonight? The guy didn't have to work. He wanted to go out with another girl!"

"I'm sorry, Ruby."

"Why? You shouldn't be sorry. *You* aren't out with anybody either. You're like I am. You're ugly. And that's why you like Helen. She likes you and makes you feel wanted."

"You aren't ugly, Ruby," I protested.

"Hu-h! Tell that to the sea gulls. I'm not scolding you, Allan. You're a nice kid. It isn't everybody who'd take a chance on drowning, just to save somebody else."

"Ruby. Let's go for a walk."

"Let me alone. I want to drink. Let me talk to you. Nobody else will listen to me. I'm not drunk, if that's what you think."

"You will be if you drink any more."

"No, I won't. And I have money. And I know the bootlegger Helen buys this stuff from."

She took a giant swig and I frowned at her. Through the excitement of watching her, I drank some of mine. It was like liquid fire in my throat. The party continued in this vein until Ruby began to talk incoherently. I didn't know how to cope with her, and by nine o'clock I wouldn't have dared

64

take her outside. She was loud and profane. She admitted sexual promiscuity, and accused herself of being a loose, oversexed girl.

Frankly, I was frightened. When she dropped a glass half-full of liquor, and fell in a limp heap, I was at my wit's end. After picking up the glass and the ice, I carried her to Carol's room.

Stretched out upon the bed she looked like she was dead. The most I felt safe to remove were her shoes. I stayed with her for several minutes but she was out cold. I straightened up the living room, wiped up as much sin as possible, then took the dirty glasses to the kitchen.

Just at that moment there were voices outside, and the tones were strong enough for me to hear what was going on.

"...You think what you please." That was Jim talking.

"Just don't bother to come around here any more!" Helen retorted.

"You've made it clear enough," Jim again. "There's one sure thing about it. The only man you'll ever get is some old buzzard about to drop dead!"

"I can get men younger than you!" she blasted back at him.

"Go get them!"

The door opened and slammed. Helen stood there, gazing fixedly at me. Then she went to the living room and dropped her purse on the table, and when she started back I could see she was weaving somewhat drunkenly.

"Did you hear that ass talking?" she asked.

"I heard somebody talking, but I didn't hear what was said," I lied.

65

"The only man I could get is somebody ready to drop dead! Of all the goddamn nerve!" She dropped into a chair. "Can you imagine something like that?"

"That's something," I agreed.

"Well," she said, "that's over with. He's completely out of my system now."

"You'll probably be happier."

She nodded and asked,

"How long did Ruby stay?"

"She's still here."

"Where?" and she glanced around.

"I put her on Carol's bed. She got pretty sick."

"You drank her under the table?"

"No, I didn't try. She wasn't feeling very good about life. She's troubled way down deep, somehow."

"Did you have her, Allan?"

"Oh, no! She wasn't troubled about that."

"That's what you think! I'll go see how she is. Put some whiskey and coke in a glass for me, baby. I'll calm down after a while."

I began thinking seriously about what she'd called me. It bothered me that she had so glibly asked such a personal question. When I'd returned from the kitchen with ice and glasses, Helen was back.

"You're a funny kid, Allan," she said, plopping down in a chair. "It was there if you'd wanted to take it. Ruby's hotter than any girl ought to be."

She looked at me when I handed her the drink. It was like an accusation that I'd really done something with Ruby.

"Doesn't Ruby appeal to you?"

"Ruby's nice, and I feel sorry for her," I said,

66

sitting down. "She didn't tell me she wanted me to do anything. She said she felt reckless."

"Women aren't supposed to tell you, Allan. She must've told you something about herself—if she got drunk enough to pass out."

My ears burned and my eyes smarted. With all Ruby had said, and all I'd seen while she'd wantonly exposed herself, I hadn't become upset. But for Helen to merely talk suggestively or look affectionately at me, brought a sensation that stirred me emotionally.

"Didn't she tell you anything?" she pursued.

"Yes. She told me her father spoiled her rotten."

"What else?"

"She said she knew a bootlegger, and could buy more whiskey."

"What else?"

"I don't remember anything else of importance."

"You have a tight mouth, Allan," and she took a swallow from her glass. "You see, I know Ruby like a book. She confides in me all the time. I've known her since my girl was a baby."

"It's nice to have old friends," I said. "Not old friends, but friends for a long time."

"You'd make any woman a good consort," she said. "I'll bet you wouldn't be proud if you had every woman in the world."

"There's a lot of women in the world. What's a consort?"

"Just a partner," she said lightly. "I'll bet if you had an affair with a woman, nobody could knock the truth out of you."

"I guess."

CHAPTER NINE

When a dumbell is in the crowd you can figure that at least *somebody* won't get the drift. I was convinced by Helen's conversation that she still suspected I'd had intimate relations with Ruby. She continued to drink, but she remained sober enough to limit the amount of whiskey that went into my drinks.

Now and then a dizziness seized me, but I wasn't drunk. The physical attraction for Helen grew and it became a problem without a solution to me. Ten minutes of silence had passed, and her glass had become empty, when she said,

"You would've helped Ruby, Allan."

"Helped her?"

"Yes. You and she could've been together and you'd never have told. It's hard for a woman to find a man she can trust."

"I never felt that way about Ruby," I objected.

"Have you ever felt that way about *any* woman?" she quizzed, frowning deeply.

"Yes, and I'm ashamed!"

"Why?" she asked. "It's nothing to be ashamed of."

"If you knew who it was, you wouldn't blame me for being ashamed."

"I'd never *blame* you," she said. "All I'm trying to tell you is that it's normal for you to feel that way."

"About you?" I asked, speaking before I thought.

"Yes, Allan, even about me."

Nervously I took a sip of my drink then said,

"I didn't intend to tell you that!"

"I knew already," she said. "Let me explain

68

Allan, about Ruby. I'm her only confidant. She's been brought up without a mother, and almost without affection. When she was very young, she trusted a boy, believed him when he told her he cared for her. After he got her started they broke up and he married. Ruby's sexually weak and she can't help it."

"That's too bad!"

"It indeed is," she echoed. "I don't want you to think unkindly of Ruby. And I don't think you're the kind of boy who would."

"I think she's nice. She can't help the way she is. She needs to get married."

"All single women need to get married," she said. "But a woman can't just get married when she wants to. She has to find a willing man, one who can provide for her."

Of course I couldn't marry Ruby, nor could I provide for her. But for some reason her problems fell onto my shoulders, and it seemed I'd been a heel for not having had gumption enough to discern her needs. But while I'd learned about Ruby, I had also realized Helen's needs. It was like when a man calls you a name, and you're what he calls you, and you don't know what to do about it.

"Allan," she said, unsteady in her chair, "some boys have inhibitions about things of this sort. At your age, some of them feel they want to remain pure for one certain girl. Is that your idea?"

"No. I just don't take to everybody that comes along."

"Look, Allan," and she got up. "We'll leave Ruby where she is. You take my bed, and I'll sleep on the sofa."

"Let me sleep on the sofa."

"All right," and she laughed. "I'll get something to put under you."

Briefly I paced the floor, like Jim had done. An unrest had settled in me, far worse than any time before. Make no mistake about it, I was infatuated with Helen, and I was deeply shaken up for having revealed it to her. Only shortly before that night, I'd had few problems: to survive and to further my education. That was changed. Sworn to secrecy, I'd kept the truth from Helen about knowing her daughter. I couldn't, later on, even tell Carol about the imtimate conversations between Helen and me.

I stood still while Helen made the sofa into a bed for me. I didn't want her to sense any inward disturbance. When she'd finished she said,

"There! You'll sleep just as well."

I might never have left Helen's house that night had she not made that one last gesture. She turned squarely to face me, and she put both her arms around my neck. Automatically my arms flew around her, the way I'd held Carol. We kissed and, for an instant, I believed she was Carol, that I was being taught how to kiss a girl. When she withdrew her arms I did likewise. She said, very softly,

"You're a good boy, Allan!"

Her movement was rapid and she was gone from the room before I returned to reality. I wanted to follow her, ask her what the kiss actually meant. Or perhaps tell her that I'd kissed Carol, ask her which of them I should romantically pursue. But I was no different that night from any other. My false modesty and my ignorance had me snowed under.

I killed the lights and sat down. There was a faint stream of light coming in from a side window, nearest to Speedway. My thoughts centered on the thirty or so dollars I'd saved, and my eyes followed the light. Shortly, my feet began to itch and I stood. It took plenty of nerve to steal into the night, yet, it would've taken more nerve to face Helen the next morning.

I was conscious that I'd left something behind. Friends. I had enough decency to remain in the area until the next day, to say goodbye to Ken. And, as I'd gone inland, my better judgment prompted me to send Helen a letter. My stopping point became Redlands, some seventy miles from the beach.

As the month of August went by, temptation gnawed at me, something told me to go back. That wasn't enough, nor was the struggle to survive, which I encountered. Many people were without electricity and gas, because they couldn't afford it. The depression had its grip around their neck and it wouldn't let go. Some families drew commodities from relief agencies, while others weren't eligible.

Everywhere hope and despair were bed partners. Hope had you through life, and despair grabbed you when hope walked out. As for myself, I'd have starved to death, even with money in my pocket. I refused to spend the last—a fear of insecurity. I gathered nickels and dimes by sweeping floors, washing windows, piling scrap iron, and a dozen other menial chores.

September came. And I saw boys and girls on their way to school. It forever gave me a feeling of nostalgia. I pictured Carol boarding the bus, then I'd see her naked, with Jim Darwin playing with her. Often times Helen and Ruby dominated the illusion. My pity for Ruby never ceased to haunt me. Helen

71

always stood majestically in my mind, and I'd feel her lips touching mine.

Except for the past one thinks of so often, life became more interesting as the word 'challenge' entered my vocabulary. When I made a dime by working, I compared the feat with that of the guy who stood on the corner, begging. There were so many things I had to be thankful for. Unlike some boys who were sixteen, I was husky, and disgustingly healthy, and nobody was afraid to give me something to lift.

By the time cold weather set in, I'd exchanged 'out' sleeping for a room in a flop house. It cost me seventy-five cents a week. As soon as the smudge pots ceased to burn, I got a job picking oranges at so much a box. When you're as thrifty as I was, you couldn't lose at a job like that. It was only seasonal but I piled up the dough.

In new surroundings, no matter how shy you are, you eventually accumulate friends. However, those friends I met were not of school age. And I found myself learning new ways of life, and discovering that Helen had been so right.

Fortunately, I didn't let anybody interfere with my making an honest living. Always, in the back of my mind, the intent to return to the beach was my foremost thought. Yet, the year rolled by, then another year, another, until six years had separated me from that part of my past.

I'd become very car conscious, and had managed by trading time after time, to own a fairly late model car. Only then did I decide to take a trip to the beach. I had expected to find things as I'd left them, everyone living in the same houses, doing the same things, and feeling the same way about life. Though I'd kept in writing touch with Ken, it seemed best to contact him before doing anything else.

He didn't live in the same place. A neighbor informed me they had moved a month ago, and gave me a fairly accurate location of their new home. It was on the street running parallel to Pacific, between the ocean and the canals. I found the place, but there was nobody home.

I drove back to the Speedway and parked in front of Carol's house. The shades were drawn, and the house looked run-down. Like a jack-in-a-box I sprang from the car and made a dash to the door, then knocked heavily. It was more than two minutes before somebody answered. It was a man and he frowned.

"Is Carol or Helen Devon here?" I asked.

"You have your houses mixed up," he said.

"Didn't they *used* to live here?"

"I can't say. They don't live here now."

I left the porch and he closed the door simultaneously. Something in my stomach turned over several times, and I felt sick. My suspicions led me to consider the possibility that the man had lied to me, that maybe he'd married Helen and didn't want any visitors.

I recalled that Helen had once mentioned that she managed a clothing store. Possibly it was in Venice, I thought. With heavy feet I climbed into my car and drove off. On my way to Venice, nothing looked the same. The houses needed painting, and there was debris scattered over the streets. I curbed in on Winward Avenue, not too far from a women's apparel shop.

From store to store I turned up nothing but negative nods. Nobody ever heard of Helen Devon. I was told that many stores had changed hands, and

73

some were either vacant or were occupied by other businesses. So it was possible that Helen's job went the way a fist goes when a hand opens.

It was nearly five o'clock when I stopped in a small restaurant for a cup of coffee. Some frilly-haired brunette was sitting next to me. She was half-turned from me, her eyes trained on a newspaper. Though I saw only part of her face, there was something familiar about her. Suddenly she turned her head to glance at me.

Our eyes locked for at least a minute, then she quickly turned again to look at her paper.

"Ruby," I said.

She started instantly.

"Remember me?" I asked.

"No," she said.

"If you're the right girl, I met you at Helen Devon's house."

"Recently?"

"No. Maybe five or six years ago."

"What's your name?"

"Allan West."

"I'm sorry, I can't seem to place you. Where did Helen live then?"

"On the beach. You came over one Saturday, and she went out with Jim Darwin. You and I were alone most of the evening."

She glanced around to see if anybody had heard me.

"I remember Jim Darwin," she said. "But I was over at Helen's house so many times, and I met so many people..."

"It's not that important," I said.

"But it is, really," she contradicted. "It embarrasses me not to remember someone who re-

74

members me!"

"Where does Helen live now?" I asked.

"Near Ocean Park."

"Did she get married?"

"Yes. And she got divorced."

"She living alone now?"

"Practically. Carol's living with her. Did you know her?"

"No. Did *she* ever get married?"

"Who'd have her?"

"Did Helen marry Jim?"

"No, thank God. She married some guy who owned a department store—three or four of them, in fact. But that didn't last. Did you get married?"

"No."

"I wish I could remember you!"

"Did you get married?" I asked her.

"Yes." and she sighed. "And I got a divorce, too. I'm on the loose again."

"Are you and Helen still friendly?"

"Surely, why not? She's the only friend I have."

"Would you like to go with me to see her?"

"I'll go with you. I have to pick up some things first," and she glanced at her watch. "I'm having some alterations done on some things I bought."

"Did your dad see the bill yet?"

"So you remember a standard joke? Daddy died last year."

"I'm very sorry!"

"Thanks. Wait a few minutes for me—I'll see if my things are ready."

She slid off the stool and left. She'd changed very little, perhaps she was fleshier and had a more pronounced walk. I had changed more than I'd realized, and seeing Ruby seemed to confirm

75

it. Now I felt an attraction for her.

CHAPTER TEN

Ruby had a late model car and she suggested she drive us over. We'd scarcely left Venice when she said,

"I remember you now!"

"Good."

"You were the beach maverick."

"Is that what Helen called me?"

"No. I called you that. You're the guy who saved Helen's life."

"How come you suddenly remembered?"

"I remembered Helen that day, when she was over her head in water, like she's over her head now with Carol. What had me fooled is your size! God, you look like a giant now, compared to then. How tall are you?"

"Six-four."

"I'll bet you really slap the girls around!"

I didn't comment and, after a full minute had elapsed, I said,

"What goes with Carol?"

"You should ask what *doesn't* go with her. She keeps the house full of tramps most of the time, and she runs around with just anything with pants on."

"Does she run around with Jim Darwin?" I asked.

"No. She probably would if he were around. Nobody's heard from or about Jim for many years."

Almost at that moment she pulled to a stop in front of a large house, practically surrounded with

76

foliage.

"This is it," she announced. "I don't see Helen's car, hope she's here."

She alighted from the car and came around to meet me, walking ahead until we stepped upon the porch, then she stood beside me and said,

"Push the buzzer. I'm going to stand back and see the surprise on her face when she sees you."

I pushed the button, wondering what would happen if Carol should answer instead of Helen. Eagerly I touched the button again.

"Just a minute! Just *one* minute!" somebody said from inside. "I'm coming!"

The door opened and Carol peered at me through the screen. Instantly she smiled, a surprised, pleased look on her face. The only difference about her was she'd lost her oval, baby-like face, and she was filled out more. I didn't want to greet her by name, and I hoped she wouldn't speak mine. What saved the situation was that Ruby shuffled her feet against the porch floor.

Carol opened the screen, and I had to step back. She gazed at Ruby and frowned.

"What's the matter, Ruby?" she asked. "Are you afraid to show yourself?"

"No," she said. "I didn't know if you'd answer, or if Helen would. This is Allan West, a friend of your mother's."

"Hello, Allan West," Carol said, sarcastically.

"Hello, Carol," I said, pushing back farther from the door.

"Is Helen here?" Ruby asked.

"No," and Carol stepped to the porch and let the screen close. "And I haven't the slightest idea when she'll be back. She doesn't tell me

77

much these days."

"What do you say, Allan, should we wait?" Ruby asked.

"Maybe Carol wouldn't care to have us wait."

"Don't be so presumptuous, Mr. West," she said. "Mother has her friends and I have mine. If you want to wait for her, you certainly may."

"Let's wait a while," Ruby suggested.

"Okay by me," I said.

Carol pulled open the door and motioned us inside.

"Just flop anywhere," she said. "I'd be happy to furnish Mother's guests with something to drink."

"Like what?" Ruby asked, noticing Carol's odd look at me.

"Anything you wish," she replied. "I might even stir up some punch," and she raised her head, tilting her chin, then smiled vaguely at me.

"Punch!" Ruby said, simulating a gagging person.

"*You* like punch, don't you, Mr. West?" Carol asked.

"Of course I do," I said. "Just anything at all is fine with me."

"Carol," Ruby said, "please don't give *me* any punch!"

She laughed as she left us. Ruby winked at me as if to say, "See what I mean?" But I shrugged it off, wishing I could talk with Carol alone.

Carol brought several brands of whiskey, some gin, ice and mixes, I thought it was very decent of her, and I was wondering what she thought of Ruby saying that I was her mother's friend. Had her mother told her about me?

78

From where I was sitting I watched Carol mix the drinks, three of them. She hadn't asked what either of us wanted, and she was pouring Scotch into the glasses. I didn't like Scotch and, when she added soda, I knew some guest was in for trouble.

"We have no servant this afternoon," Carol said. "So come and get your own drinks!"

I rose quickly, reached the table, and took two drinks, one for Ruby, the other for myself.

"Thank you, Carol," I said.

"Don't mention it," she said. "I've wanted a drink all afternoon, but I didn't want to drink by myself."

That was something, I thought, as I handed Ruby her drink. Our being there offered some help to her. I sat again, watching Carol's tiny figure sink into a deep arm chair. She threw one leg over one of the arms, and began swinging her foot.

There was an ominous quiet, while Carol glanced at the ceiling, like she wished we weren't there. I tasted the drink and it was horrible. I must have frowned for Carol said,

"Don't like it, eh?"

"Frankly, no," I said.

"There's the stuff," she pointed. "Go get what you want. I'm a poor hostess, at best."

I rose, set my glass on the table and returned to my seat.

"Don't you want anything else?" Carol asked.

"No, thanks anyhow."

"I'll fix you something, Allan," Ruby offered.

"Nothing," I said. "I can go without drinking."

"I take it you're temperamental," Carol surmised.

"You might be a poor hostess," Ruby said, but you don't have to be so nasty!"

"Nasty people, nasty hostess," Carol said lazily. "If the guy wants something, he's welcome to it."

"Is it all right for me to use your bathroom, Carol?" Ruby asked.

"For God's sake, Ruby!" Carol said impatiently. "You know where it is, and you know you're welcome to whatever's here. Did you people come here with a chip on your shoulder?"

"Let's go back to the porch and start all over again," I suggested. "Something happened—we must've done something wrong when we came in."

"Aw, skip it," Carol said. "Go ahead, Ruby, and don't act like a child."

Ruby shrugged and got up, leaving her drink on the end table beside her chair. She went silently to the bathroom, leaving Carol to stare at me.

"You bastard!" she said, leaning forward. "Why'd you have to go shack up with my mother after I left?"

"Who told you I shacked up with her?" I asked, amused.

"She practically admitted it! But you found it convenient to scram, just before I got back!"

"That was safer than waiting for you to get there," I said.

"You're damn right it was! It's a good thing you did scram. Did somebody tell you I'd left again? Cr were you intending to shack up with her again, whether I'm gone or not?"

"I hadn't decided. I hear you're doing a lot of shacking yourself these days."

"If that crummy bitch you're with told you that,

you can discount it. My body's only one tempera-
ture and *that's* cold!''

She fell back into the chair when we heard Ruby
coming back.

"You like coke and whiskey, don't you, Allan?"
Ruby asked, stopping at the mixing table.

"I do."

"Mix him something potent," Carol suggested.

"I think you're taking Allan the wrong way,"
Ruby said. "He's really a swell guy. He's the
one who saved your mother from drowning."

"I've had six years in which to appreciate
that," Carol said. "Now, Allan, I'll tell you.
Thanks for saving my mother's life."

"Your mother thanked me a long time ago," I
said.

"Where're you living, Allan?" Carol asked.

"About seventy miles inland," I said, taking
the drink Ruby handed me.

"Do you plan on moving back to the beach?"

"No."

"He will if I can persuade him," Ruby said.

"And if I know you," Carol said, "you'll do
the job okay!"

"I think after we finish our drinks we'd better
go, Ruby," I said. "I have to see another friend
before it gets too late. Maybe I can see Helen the
next time I come."

"When will that be?" Carol asked.

"I don't know."

"Mother'll be terribly disappointed about missing you," she said. "She goes inland quite often
—maybe if you left your address..."

"It's 3870 Colton Avenue, Redlands," I told
her.

She jumped from her chair, got a pencil and wrote it down. Then she repeated it, to see if she had it correctly.

"Let me have the pencil and some paper," Ruby said. "I want to get it down too. Sometimes I go inland."

Rather annoyed, Carol tore off the address and handed Ruby the remaining half of the sheet of paper. While Ruby was writing, the doorbell rang. Carol strutted to the door and opened it. A girl-faced boy was framed behind the screen, and he smiled broadly at Carol.

"Come in, Gerald," she said.

I got up and so did Ruby. Gerald came in and Carol began introducing him to me. I took a strong grasp on the guy's hand and gave it a firm shake. He got the impression that I was one of Ruby's boy friends, and he didn't seem unhappy because I was there.

"We'll be seeing you, Carol!" Ruby said.

"Okay," she said. "You come back, Allan. I know Mother'll be glad to see you."

I smiled at her and she tried to talk with her eyes, which I made an effort to ignore. Six years hadn't changed my opinion of her, yet I was still convinced that she was out of my class, financially if nothing else. Since I was slow in leaving, Ruby took my hand and urged me out. When we were in the car she said,

"I think Carol went for you."

"She goes for Gerald too," I said.

"And plenty of others. What'll we do now?"

"Go back to my car. Then you can have the rest of the evening for whatever you care to do."

"What if I don't care to do anything?"

82

"Whatever you think."

"You were just kidding about seeing that friend, weren't you?"

"No. I do want to see a friend."

"Let me take you to see him, then we'll do something. It's been six years since I've seen you."

I smiled, recalling that she hadn't remembered me. But I thought her idea was good, as I figured it'd help keep my mind off Carol.

"All right," I agreed. "Shove off, and go down Pacific Avenue."

As Ruby stepped on the gas, I glanced back to see Carol peering out the window. I believed then I'd be much safer back in Redlands, as the distance between there and the Coast did a lot for my occasional bad notions.

Ken's mother was there, and she told me he'd left two days ago to work in Long Beach. It was disappointing but I chatted with her, assuring her that I was getting on all right. When I returned to Ruby's car and announced that my friend wasn't home, her face lit up and she sighed, pretending to be sorry. Again we were rolling, and I left the rest up to her.

CHAPTER ELEVEN

Ruby had one of those duplex affairs. You entered the front room from the porch, and the quarters stretched to the rear of the building, the bedroom situated in the farthest part. It was nice, well-furnished, and immaculately clean. Without an invitation I sank into a chair, while she took her parcels to her bedroom.

I remembered that Helen had been in sympathy with Ruby's nature, and had practically admonished me for not having taken Ruby. Things were different now; my nature was mature, and I tried to tell myself that I'd be doing Ruby a favor if a fling availed itself, and I participated.

I saw her enter the kitchen, as I could see all the way back to the bathroom door, next to the bedroom. The refrigerator door slammed and I could hear her tugging with an ice tray. Before long she came in with two giant highballs.

"I'd like to get you drunk," she announced, passing me the glass. "The last time, you held back and I got soused. And I forgot to tell you. Helen was almost out of her mind when she finally decided you weren't coming back."

"You're remembering more all the time," I said.

"I remember something else too," she cooed.

"That I was real stupid?"

"Maybe, and maybe not. But Helen liked you more than you might've thought, and *not* necessarily as a *mother* should!"

"You let your imagination run away with you," I said.

"It wasn't *my* imagination! Helen told me how she felt about you."

I reminisced those hours I'd spent with Helen, and recalled my feelings for her. But now, as I sat in Ruby's apartment, I was glad nothing more had come of it. With Ruby it would've been quite different, had I wanted and had her that night.

Ruby took a place on the sofa and said,

"Sit with me, over here."

I moved to her side and from that moment it was

84

fun. It was an advantage to know Ruby's nympho-
maniacal tendencies but the knowledge was taking
its toll. Already I was fighting with the aggres-
siveness that it engendered. Though she appealed
to me, I knew she wasn't the girl I would want to
marry some day. For that reason I didn't want
to make passes at her, to obligate myself in any
way.

"I like you very much, Allan," she said.

"I like you more than I did the other time," I
said. "I guess it's because I'm more grown-up
now."

"We both are grown-up more, but I guess I'm
not much different than I was then. I don't feel
as sorry for myself, but I'm still just as passionate. I've already wished a lot of times this evening
that I'd been sober enough that night to remember
what it was like with you. When we didn't hear
from you, and you didn't come back, I worried for
a whole month that I might've gotten pregnant."

"I didn't have anything to do with you that
night," I denied.

"You didn't?" and she looked surprised.

"No. Don't women even know when they've
done something like that?"

"Apparently they don't, if you say we didn't do
anything."

"Well, we didn't, and I'm surprised you're remembering things now that didn't even happen.
At first you didn't remember me at all."

"I see you're not going to forgive me for that,"
she said poutingly. "It wasn't because I've been
with so many men I can't remember all of them."

"I wouldn't accuse you of that," I said.

"I'm pretty loose, Allan, because I'm very

85

passionate. But I don't go out with just anybody who comes along. I wouldn't have let you pick me up if you hadn't known my name, and told me Helen's name, and all that."

"I'm not accusing you of being loose. I feel differently from what you might think. If you want to be with a man, that's your business."

"I'll bet you don't have any respect for a girl after you've had her."

"If I have respect for her before, I'll have respect for her afterwards."

She seemed pleased. She clinked her glass against mine and winked at me when I looked into her eyes. She was very pretty, and nobody (but a goof ball like I'd once been) would've turned down a possibility to exchange love with her.

"You know, Allan," she said, "if I drink too much, I either don't remember what it's like with somebody, or I'm not up to par enough to do my part. I won't have to drink and drink, trying to get you drunk, before we could do something, will I?"

"No. But I'll have to tell you, Ruby, I don't love you. And if we play around, I want to be able to leave, just like the guy does who comes downstairs after he's paid a girl."

"I won't try to hook you, Allan. I'll never try to hold you. You'll always be free to go when you want to. Just don't go and tell other guys about me."

"That goes without asking," I promised.

"Will you stay?" she asked.

"Yes."

"You know what we ought to do?"

"What?"

"Go out and eat. Then go after your car. We can

86

come back here, and we'll be free to just live! And in the morning, I'll make breakfast here."

"Sounds good."

She turned her lips toward me, and I leaned and kissed them as softly as I could. Her eyes closed and she held herself there, inviting me to kiss her many times, which I did, enjoying it very much. When she finally opened her eyes she said,

"That meant a lot to me. The way you did it."

It's peculiar how you can be trapped without a trapper. All you need is a trap. That evening and night with Ruby was my first experience in such luxury. After we'd eaten, and I'd driven my car back to her house, we'd resumed drinking, but in a more comfortable fashion. I was shirtless and shoeless, and Ruby was casually lounging in a thin kimona.

She wasn't an exhibitionist, nor was she in any sense brazen. She kept her kimona closely tied and not once during our lounging did she reveal even a hint of her cleavage. She began to grow on me, while my ignorance led me to believe that only fascination had snared me. I had a strong desire to touch her, to cup her breasts, to kiss her like I had earlier that evening. I thought that my anxiety was due to a well-planned, anticipated evening.

Fighting with myself for almost an hour made me nervous and edgy. Instead of pawing Ruby, I downed my drink and rattled what ice was left in the glass.

"I'll make you another drink," she said, rising instantly.

"How about you?"

"I'll have another one, too."

While I paced the floor, my hands deep in my pockets, I reminded myself that Ruby was quite well off and, like Carol, was out of my class. With Ruby, however, there was some difference. I didn't consider, nor had I contemplated nor entertained, a future with Ruby. Silently but firmly I admonished myself for even thinking of anything more than a night and an affair with Ruby.

She brought the drinks and very calmly returned to her place on the lounge. I didn't sit, but she kept out of my inner conflict. Finally, when I felt the situation was getting out of hand, I suggested,

"Perhaps I'd better not stay after all."

"For God's sake, why?" and she rose to confront me.

"I don't know. I'm getting nervous." And I took a large gulp of the coke and whiskey.

"Allan," she put her hand on my shoulder, "you know very well what's wrong with you!"

"No, I don't!" I said much too loudly.

"Then, I'll tell you. Sit down with me."

We both sat and she took my arm and put it around her shoulders.

"The same thing that's wrong with me," she said. "You've lived a lonely life, and you need love. And to get love, sometimes you have to give it. Haven't you wanted to put your arm around me."

"Yes."

"Why didn't you?"

"I don't know....No, I *do* know. I didn't want to make up to you. It seemed too insincere."

"You wanted me to do all of it?"

"I guess."

"My mouth is much more aggressive than my

body, Allan. I can talk, hint, and act like a common trollop, but it's no good. I can't physically seduce you."

I took another long drink, while my arm still lay limp across her shoulders.

"Make me believe you *want* me, Allan, even if it's only for just this one time. I can respond to whatever you do, but you *must* make some attempt."

I got up and started walking around the room. She was watching me, obviously so, waiting for me to come to some definite decision. Gulps from the glass became more frequent and soon it was empty again.

"Here," she said, getting up again. "I'll get you another one."

"Why aren't you drinking?" I asked.

"Right now, I don't need it as badly as you do. You need to loosen up, relax, and forget morals and conventions, and perhaps a few ideals too."

"You said it!" and I began rubbing the nape of my neck.

"Let me get the drink," she said soothingly.

She took the glass and left. I watched her walk, and her undulating body was most disturbing. *Now! Go to her! I* told myself. *Take her around the waist and hug her to you.* But I couldn't. She returned in a moment and I nervously grasped the fresh drink. Calmly she sat again and I envied her state of mind.

"Sit beside me?" she asked.

I did as she asked. One hand rested on her lap. I found it and squeezed tightly. With ample pressure she reciprocated and said,

"You must work hard—your hand is rough."

89

"Yes."

She turned her face to me and my lips moved toward it. The position was awkward but my pulse quickened,. and both of our mouths opened to a more expansive kiss. I pulled away, let go of her hand, then took her drink from her. Hurriedly I put both glasses on the rug and gathered her into my arms.

"Allan! You feel so good!"

"So do you," I said.

Again our lips met and, still holding the kiss, I drew her to a reclining position on the sofa. What followed was tensely exciting and I forgot that I didn't love Ruby. Deeper and deeper I fell into her encircling passion, and bolder and bolder came her reciprocation to my ardent caresses.

Time became suspended. Nothing was urgent. But at the same moment I knew of two people lost in a great pool of furious emotion, Ruby and myself. Things were happening and I wasn't sure I was one of the two at the controls. Regardless of my lack of experience, the whole thing was like second nature, an instinct which guides one through the darkness.

The catch came, the possible trap, when minutes later I discovered the absence of disgust I'd previously felt after such intimacy. There was a gnawing hunger lurking in my heart, and I was holding Ruby more tightly than anytime before. It was like when you get up from the table, still hungry, and you're reluctant to leave anything behind. So, I continued to hold her, nestling my cheek against hers.

CHAPTER TWELVE

A dissonant sound began piercing my ear drums and I tried to awake. I vaguely recalled later that I had wrapped my head in a pillow, trying to delay awakening to the terrible ringing of the buzzer. Finally, when I'd given up, I roused Ruby from a deep sleep.

"Ruby! Ruby! Somebody's ringing your door-bell!"

"My God," she said sleepily. "Go see who it is."

"Christ, no!" I blurted.

"All right," she said, "I'll go."

While she slid out of bed and got her kimona, the impatient buzzer kept on. I hurried to dress, and my head seemed three sizes larger than normal. Then I heard a familiar voice.

"Didn't have anything in particular to do this morning. Thought I'd drop in."

"I'm glad you did," I heard Ruby say. "I was asleep. Sit down and I'll make some coffee for you."

Nothing else was said just then, but I heard Ruby in the kitchen. The voice was unmistakably Carol's, and I had a good idea how I'd feel if she discovered that I'd slept with Ruby.

There was no way I could get to the bathroom without Carol seeing me. The room had just one door and a window provided my only escape. Using Ruby's hair brush and comb, I tried to manage my hair to a less disheveled state, then angled to the window.

91

However, for some reason, Ruby had different ideas. I was already opening the window when she called out:

"The coffee's almost ready, Allan!"

The floor under me was solid, otherwise I might have fallen through. I had a sudden feeling of fear and, for the first time I trembled. It didn't dawn on me then that Ruby was using her cunning to queer me with both Carol and Helen.

"Where is the guy?" I heard Carol say.

"In the bedroom," Ruby replied. "Allan! The coffee's ready!"

I wanted to choke her. I still hadn't decided to come out when Carol stuck her head into the room.

"What's going on, lug?" she asked.

"You make it around pretty early, don't you?" I asked.

"Somehow I knew you'd be here!" she said, coming on in. Then she breathed a loud whisper, "you're worse than a bastard!"

"You call me that one more time, and I'll slap you silly!" I told her.

"You wouldn't dare!" she said, with an evil smile.

I brushed past her and went to the kitchen. Ruby beamed at me and I scowled at her. Carol followed practically on my heels, and she said,

"This setup's real cozy. Did you know, Ruby, that Allan and I were pretty thick before I took that last trip to Rhode Island?"

Ruby was pouring coffee and she set down the pot and whirled to face Carol with a look of disbelief, then she finally focused her attention upon me.

"I thought you didn't know Carol?"

92

"What difference does it make?" I asked unkindly.

"No difference at all, Allan. But why did you hide it?"

"For the same reason I would've hidden this— my being here with you—if you hadn't given it away. Whose business is it what I do and who I know?"

"Allan's very gallant," Carol said. "He goes from one girl to another, and keeps their secrets as well as his own. He can have more girls that way."

"It sounds dirty the way you say it," I told her. "Once you asked me not to tell anybody about us."

"Sure I did," she admitted. "But in those days I cared. Now I don't. After you shacked up with mother, what do I care what *she* thinks? She was old enough to be *your* mother. In fact," and she nodded toward Ruby, "*she's* pretty old for you."

"Well," Ruby sighed, picking up the coffee pot again, "let's don't argue about it. I'm sure Allan will make his choice without our help."

"Sure," and Carol sat at the table. "Mother'll probably be over here after a while—that'll give give him three of us to choose between. Do you have any sugar, Ruby?"

"Yes," and Ruby refilled the sugar bowl and pushed it toward Carol.

"Thank you, dear Ruby. Want sugar in your coffee, Romeo?"

"I'll put it in," I said.

Ruby sat, then motioned for me to sit. Carol smiled smugly at me. I tried to ignore her, even tried to think of something to slur back at her. I

93

guess I was built wrong—I'd already forgiven her for being catty.

"If it means anything now, Allan," Carol said, stirring her coffee, "I've been sorry a lot of times about going to Rhode Island. I was sorry right after I'd left, and more than sorry when I returned and found you gone."

"It wasn't so bad up there after Jim Darwin got there, was it?" I asked.

She nearly spilled a mouthful of coffee. But she quickly regained her poise and broke into a laugh. I hadn't denied that I'd shacked up with her mother, and I was curious to see if she'd deny my accusation.

"I guess Mother was pretty worried about that," she said. "Poor Mother! Did you worry too, Allan?"

"Nope."

"Nope! You've changed. You didn't used to say things like that. Is Jim the reason you left before I got back?"

"No."

"Well, Jim wasn't really too old for me—it was just that I was too young then for a man his age. I'm sorry, though, that the possibility caused you and Mother so much doubtful worry."

"Isn't there something else to talk about?" Ruby asked.

"I'm sorry, Ruby," I said.

"I am too, Ruby," Carol apologized insincerely. "But it did hurt my pride that Allan didn't wait for me to come back. You understand how I feel, don't you?"

"Of course," Ruby acknowledged. "Would you have breakfast with us, Carol?"

94

"Ate already," she said. "You know how early I get up!"

"Yes," Ruby said wanly.

The doorbell buzzed again and Carol said,

"That's mother, I'll bet. Want me to let her in?"

"Would you, Carol?" Ruby asked.

"Surely!"

I dreaded facing Helen but I looked at Ruby and shrugged.

"You didn't really shack with Helen, did you, Allan?"

"Of course I didn't."

"With Carol?"

"No!"

Then Helen came in and I got up, intending to shake her hand, but she rushed up and threw her arms around me.

"It's so good to see you, Allan!" she said happily.

"Thank you," I said, my lips against her hair. "It's good to see you too, Helen."

We broke apart and Ruby rose.

"Hello, Helen," Ruby said. "Sit down and I'll get you a cup of coffee."

"Thank you, dear," and Helen sat down. "I thought you were going to Long Beach today, Carol."

"I changed my mind, Mother. I decided to come over here and see my old beau again."

"Your what?"

"My old *beau*. Perhaps Allan didn't tell you that he and I were *very close* before I went to Rhode Island that last time."

"No, he didn't," and Helen looked at me for

95

some explanation.

"I don't talk much about other people's business," I defended.

"Which is good," Helen agreed.

"While we're on the subject," I said, "we should get something straightened out while you and Carol are together. Carol has some idea that you and I were intimate while I stayed at your house."

"For God's sake, Carol!" Helen said. "I gave you more credit than that. You get that out of your mind."

Ruby was white while she poured coffee, and Carol was looking contemplatively at me, like she hadn't heard her mother. Helen was still beautiful, and I was aware that the same old attraction for her existed. But so what? I was no less attracted to Carol; I was already sexually hooked by Ruby.

"I'll compromise," Carol said suddenly. "You convince Allan that Jim and I had nothing to do with one another, and I'll believe that you and Allan didn't shack!"

"I don't think Allan needs convincing of that," Helen said. "You'd have a harder time making him believe that something **did** exist between you and Jim."

"I don't see the necessity of anything like this," Ruby said. "I met Allan yesterday and we had fun together, and I think these things could be taken up with him some other time—when he isn't with me."

"Don't worry, Ruby," Carol said. "Nobody's going to take your Romeo away from you. You can have him. I don't need him."

"Well, I wouldn't think so!" Ruby said. "Carol, you have more guys now than you know what to do with. The past has gone by, and if it's meant for you and Allan to take up with each other again, it'll just happen."

"You make me look like a chippy, Ruby," Carol objected.

"I don't intend to, do I, Helen?"

"Of course not. I think Allan's capable of choosing his own friends, and, Carol, you and he can get together sometime and talk over old times."

"This afternoon would be a good time," Carol suggested. "Since you and Ruby had something planned for this afternoon, Allan and I can take a ride and talk."

"Certainly," Ruby said, revealing a pained expression. "If Allan wants to, why not?"

"Well?" and Carol looked at me.

"I guess."

"Well, don't fall over backwards with happiness!" she chided.

"All right!" Helen said. "It's all settled. Now set the time, and let's not hear any more about it."

"I'll be available at one o'clock," Carol said. "Shall I pick you up, Allan?"

"Fine."

Carol was anything but grim as she started to drink her coffee. Several times, during a long conversation with Helen, Ruby glared viciously at Carol. I wasn't happy with the spot I was in, and I wanted to get it over and done with.

Carol left first and immediately Helen apologized for her. When she was leaving, she reconfirmed plans with Ruby, then turned to me and said,

"Allan, Carol isn't really a bad girl. Don't think harshly of her, please. She has some idea that she should have a whack at anything she wants to try, and I think she'll pull back after you and she have talked."

"Sure!" I said. "I remember Carol. There won't be any trouble. I just let her talk, let her say whatever she wants to."

This went over very well, and after Helen left, Ruby remarked,

"Carol won't give up until she gets you!"

"Let's not worry about it, Ruby, please. You and I talked about ourselves last night—before anything happened between us."

"I know. Let's eat breakfast. I believe that was the last part of our bargain. Then, after breakfast..."

I hugged her to me and said,

"Don't make it sound so final. There'll be other times."

"Maybe," and she sighed heavily. "I made a mistake letting Carol know you were here."

"Yes, that you did!"

CHAPTER THIRTEEN

Carol was early. She sat on her horn until Ruby opened the door to tell her that we knew she'd arrived. When I started out Ruby stopped me to say,

"I'll be back home around eight, if you make it back. I don't want to tell you what to do, but if you don't come back I'll miss you."

"I'll be back," I promised, along with a light kiss on her cheek. "My car'll be here."

"The key will be under the mat if you get here first," she said.

"Thanks, Ruby."

Carol appeared impatient when I slid in beside her, but I ignored her scowl. With a heavy foot on the gas pedal, the car lunged forward, throwing me back against the cushion.

"Where'd you like to ride to?" she asked.

"I'll leave that to you, Carol."

"You always make it sound like you're agreeable and easy to get along with."

"I am."

"That's a lot of you know what!"

When I didn't comment she said,

"Want to walk on the beach?"

"All right with me."

There was nothing else said, and she drove quite sanely. When we reached the beach and left the car, her walking gait was slow and she seemed preoccupied. There were a number of people sprawled on the sand, also some swimming, and we kept to the higher section of the beach until we reached the old pier under which I'd once lived.

"You know, Allan," she said, "once I told you I was spoiled rotten?"

"I remember."

"You still liked me, didn't you?"

"Yes."

"I guess I'm worse now. Would you like to sit down on the sand?"

"Okey."

99

She dropped to the sand, and what breeze there was tossed her hair as she gazed toward the sea. I sat fairly close to her and began looking at the pier, reflecting grimly the days when the beach owned me.

"Do you like Ruby a lot?" she asked.

"She's very nice."

"You didn't answer my question, Allan."

"I don't want to answer it."

"Remember the night when I followed you, and asked you to wait for me—until I got back from Rhode Island?"

"Yes, I do."

"I almost didn't go," she revealed. "Funny. I thought that night that I was in love with you. And I used to think you were so ugly."

"Why'd you think you were in love with me?"

"I don't know. Just like I don't know why I got so burned up when I found you with Ruby this morning. Ruby's not the girl for you. She's too old for you, and I doubt that one man could ever satisfy her."

"What about you, Carol? One man doesn't seem to satisfy you."

"That's an unfair assumption," she said, casting her gaze entirely upon me.

"Maybe it's unfair to say it about Ruby, too." I avoided her eyes.

"I guess. There I go picking up your habits! You always said that, and you still do. Anyhow, how long are you going to stay?"

"I was planning to leave tonight. I'm poor, and I have to work."

"You could work here, couldn't you?"

"It'd be hard to find a job."

"I guess..." and she put her hand over her lips. "There I go again! Slap me when I say that!"

"That isn't what makes me want to slap you," I told her.

"I know," and she smiled. "I don't like it here. Let's go to my house where we can drink something."

"All right."

Carol was definitely in conflict with herself as she drove home. While I speculated about our getting together, her past and present actions were standing like a barred door before me.

Once we were in her house her attitude changed. It was almost like she had become somebody else. I had taken a comfortable chair in the front room, merely waiting to see what would happen next. Presently she had the liquor there and she began making drinks.

"I'll fix coke for you," she said. "I'm really sorry about yesterday. But honestly, I didn't know what you liked."

"Nobody got hurt," I said.

"But you didn't deserve such lousy hospitality. I guess I was too irked to be decent."

A comment didn't seem necessary, though she looked to me for one. When I saw that the drinks were ready, I rose and went to the mixing table.

"I would've brought it to you," she said.

"That's all right." I picked up the drink and tasted it.

"The way you like it?" she asked.

"Just right. Now tell me, Carol, why am I here with you?"

"You could answer that better than I can. Maybe because you want to be."

101

"We'll say I want to be, but why do *you* want me here?"

"I don't know. I'm going to get some music started. Sit down and we'll talk between tunes."

I didn't want to sit. I felt a recurrence of the nervousness I'd experienced with Ruby. She made several selections before sighing satisfaction regarding the type of music she wanted. Then, her drink in her hand, she waltzed to me, urging me to dance with her. The tips of her breasts barely brushed my chest, and it was noticeable that she avoided rubbing against me.

"You could be a good dancer," she observed. "You've grown so big and awkward, and you're stiff. Relax and swing freely."

Nothing changed except I became stiffer. She stopped, drew away from me, and said,

"You won't even try! I think you hate me, Allan!"

"I don't hate anybody. There's nothing you can tell me about my size and looks that I don't already know. Why don't you run me back to Ruby's, and you can call one of your more relaxed and handsome friends."

She moved to me, closer than she'd danced, and she tilted her chin and puckered her lips. I didn't take the hint, though I wanted very much to.

"You see," she said, "that proves you hate me. Nobody ever refuses to kiss me. And I think you're very touchy, Allan."

I reached behind her head and gathered her hair into my hand, then pulled her head closer and pressed my lips against hers. Her mouth opened, and she began breathing rather hard. For a moment I felt like crushing her half to death. Finally I

102

let her go, then turned abruptly and walked to the front window.

"Come on back," she prompted. "I promise you, Allan, I won't say another unkind word to you!"

"I don't really care what you say," I faced her again. "You don't know what you want, and neither do I. All this business between us is nothing but junk, the way ordinary kids act."

Silently she went to the table and put down her glass. She was thinking very deeply, pondering over what I'd said. Her back was to me, and I walked over and took her by her shoulders and turned her around.

"Look, Carol! You have too much. You don't need me, and I'm not the type for you anyhow. Give me a ride back to where my car is."

"No!" and she flung her arms around me, stretching her small body, standing on her toes. "I don't have as much as you think."

"You have plenty of boy friends," I said, holding her tightly.

"Yes, but what do they want? Me? Or just to have a fling with me? I'm not as dumb as they think."

Her head was on my chest and I rocked her playfully. I didn't like seeing her unhappy, and her pint-size reminded me of a little girl who was crying over a lost sucker.

"Here," I said, rubbing her cheek. "Nobody thinks you're dumb."

She looked up at me and smiled, and there were tears in her eyes. I couldn't help putting my lips to one tearful eye.

"You're a grand big lug!" she whispered.

"Don't go away again!"

I felt like picking her up and I did. After carrying her around for a few seconds, she began to laugh and kick her feet. Her elation was contagious and I felt funny all over. Rather than let my emotions race out of control, I put her down.

She took my hand and led me to the divan. She stretched out and tugged at my hand. I lay beside her, without a thought of caution. Her fingers began combing my hair, and her eyes were sort of blank as she pretended to look only at her hand going through the hair.

"Don't take advantage of me, Allan," she pleaded. "I think you're the only guy I know who could, but I feel that you won't."

"No," I said, feeling her body vibrate.

"If I tell you something, will you keep it a secret?" she asked.

"If you want me to."

"I'm secretly engaged."

"Why a secret?" I asked, a pang of jealousy touching my heart.

"Just in case it doesn't come off, nobody'll be laughing."

"Rich or poor?" I asked.

"In between, I'd say. He's a swell guy, high morals, and all."

"You're a funny girl," and I got up and sat beside her. "You take life and people much too lightly."

Then I stood, stretched lazily, and pretended indifference about what she'd told me.

"I know what you're thinking," she said. "And you're getting ready to leave." She rose and sat, pulling her skirt down over her legs. "All of this happened before you came back. And there's Ruby..."

"You're right, Carol. I *am* leaving. Let's be friends, and I won't tell your secret."

"If you insist on leaving, I'll drive you to Ruby's. And I hope you have a good time sleeping with her again tonight!"

I looked at her but she avoided my eyes. She got up and stuffed her blouse into the waist of her skirt, then went to a mirror to smooth her hair.

"Ruby's nothing but a tramp," she said. "And that's what you were, I guess, the way you lived on the beach—just a beachcomber."

She was right about me, and I saw no particular reason to argue with her by defending Ruby. I'd often heard women's appraisals of other women, and they had ceased to annoy me. I can't say, however, that her evaluation of me didn't sting.

"Ruby's probably told you a bunch of junk about me," she went on, fluffing her hair with both hands. "It's too bad you'll never know if it's true or not. Are you ready to go?"

"Yes."

She shot me a look of disgust but I grinned, somewhat amused at her attitude. I walked out first, leaving her to lock the door. Then I proceeded to the car and took my fingernail file and began cleaning my nails, hoping that I'd be calm when she climbed in. It affected her, the fact that I wasn't riled, for she said:

"That's how much you care. Digging away at your nails, like nothing in the world mattered!"

The ride back together was mantled in silence. That's the way I wanted it to be. At Ruby's I climbed out and thanked her. She drove off without saying goodbye.

CHAPTER FOURTEEN

I'd driven quite a lot that afternoon, looking over the familiar area. After deciding that driving and looking wouldn't settle anything, I went back to Ruby's house and took the key from under the mat. I don't recall the time but it was late afternoon when I entered and slumped into a chair. At the time it seemed impossible to decide whether to leave or stay. Anyhow, before too long, I fell asleep in the chair.

What awakened me might have been part of a dream, or possibly caused the dream, I don't know. But Ruby was bending over me, kissing me warmly. Subconsciously I was apparently reciprocating, for when I came to my arm was around her.

"How long have you been here?" she asked.

"I don't know," and I glanced at my watch. "Nine o'clock! I'd better get started back."

"Allan, please! Don't go back! Please *don't* go back."

"I don't want any more beachcombing," I objected, recalling Carol's remarks.

"You stay with me, Allan. Don't you care for me at all? Did Carol change your mind about me?"

"Carol changed nothing," I said, rubbing my left eye. "But I told you last night that I'd want to be able to walk away when I felt like it."

"That's your right," she said. "But I really need you now!"

"If I stayed here, both Carol and Helen would be running in and out, and Carol wouldn't stop making cracks."

"We don't have to stay here," she said. "The beach house is vacant, and we could go there. Nobody'd be running in and out. Do me this one favor, Allan. *Please?*"

I didn't answer. My hand was going slowly and thoughtfully over her back and waist, and a vivid remembrance of the night before tantalized me. I wasn't virtuous enough to refuse her. Nor was I strong enough. Her needs and desires were frank and real, while mine were suppressed. What the hell, I thought! Except that Carol had always haunted me, what was the difference between the two women?

"All right," I agreed, feigning resignation, "I'll stay for a while, Ruby."

She nearly smothered me with kisses, and I enjoyed them immensely, and I began looking forward to my stay with her. When she withdrew she stood up, extremely happy, and she said,

"We'll have fun together! I'll get some things ready and we'll spend the night over there."

The beach house was almost like any other house, except that its bay windows faced the ocean, and at high tide water washed under it. The structure was rustic, and it was situated between my former stamping grounds and Playa Del Rey. It hadn't entirely been unlived in since Ruby's father had passed on. The staples in the cupboards, the absence of dust on the furniture, and many other details, indicated that somebody had been there frequently.

That heavenly first night was wondrous and exquisite, and for the most part revealing. Ruby was no novice at love nor its many variations.

That was the night I discovered that nudity wasn't obscene, that it was our most precious art. But despite the earthiness of our association, and the almost delirious thrills and ecstasy engendered, I felt the need for something more.

Though Ruby was loaded with immediate passion and needed no aphrodisiac, she took frenzied pride in exciting me to the point of near-insanity, the results of which kept me as insatiate as she. Her methods, prompted by a possessive hope, were calculatively executed.

I awoke the following morning, nearly noon, finding Ruby gone. At first, when she wasn't in bed, it didn't disturb me. But later, after I'd roamed through the house and still hadn't found her, the impact of not having her filled me with panic. Was my reaction sane? Did I love Ruby? Had our getting together been fate? These questions and others rushed through my mind.

I returned to the bedroom, gripped by a langour dangerous to human health. Dress, something told me. Go outside and look for her car. Maybe she'd gone to buy something. That was it! I smiled and relaxed, but nonetheless I reflected the terror and and frustration I'd suffered when I awoke and she wasn't there.

Ruby came back, carrying two paper sacks of provisions. I was so glad to see her, yet I didn't dare show it. Her smile was radiant, like she'd slept alone, and she called a cheery good morning to me.

"Why didn't you wake me up?" I admonished.

"No," she said, dropping the bags on the table. "You were sleeping too soundly, I didn't want to disturb you. Get your face washed and I'll get the breakfast. You look starved!"

Suddenly I decided that this sort of thing was really living. It was a life second only to the way a king lived. That thought gave me enough energy to make the bathroom and wash. Hastily I went back to Ruby.

"Good morning!" she said, eyeing my groomed hair.

I smiled, feeling safer in her presence, knowing, however, that I wasn't.

"Did you bring any clothes with you?" she asked.

"A change, that's all," I said. "I brought swimming trunks."

"Good. I feel like a swim today. Are you happy?"

"I don't know," and I took her into my arms, her body held tight against mine. "Are you?"

"You'd better not do that, if you want any breakfast. You know by now how I am."

She was standing by the stove and I released her, reluctantly this time.

"I'm very happy right now," she added. "I could go on like this forever."

That was quite a spell, I figured. I left the the bay windows. I gazed out over the surf, then my eyes came to rest on a group of sun bathers. eyes came to rest on a group of sun bathers. Carol Devon was lying stretched out on the sand before me. Did she know I was there? Had she purposely come to that part of the beach?

There were three girls, including Carol, and three men. They were bunched so nearly together, I assumed they were all one party. For a short time I told myself that Carol wasn't on the sand;

109

that I merely *thought* I saw her. I moved away from the window, paced the livingroom floor, then went back to the kitchen. Ruby was taking eggs out of a skillet.

"Sit down, honey," she said. "These are the last of the eggs to be fried, and all I have to do is pour the coffee."

I obeyed. My appetite was weak, and I was angry at Carol. When Ruby'd poured the coffee and sat, I asked,

"Did you see Carol or Helen this morning, while you were gone?"

"Why, no. What makes you ask that?"

"Go to the window and look down on the beach. See if you know anybody down there."

She hesitated for a moment, then did as I asked. When she came back to the table her lips were firmly set.

"It's Carol and a flock of her friends," she said. "I don't know why she came this far up the beach, Allan. Honestly I don't."

"Well," I said, stabbing a fork into an egg, she's out there. Ruby, if I thought you..."

"Allan! I *did not* see Carol or Helen. I don't know why she came this far down. Will you believe me?"

"Sure. But if I ever find out differently, that's all for me."

"Don't be upset," she said. "Eat, and forget about her. Honestly, Allan, I don't know why that girl upsets you so much."

Her statement was something for me to think about and I commenced to think objectively. It was no mystery, really, why Carol upset me, it was only that I wouldn't admit the truth even to myself. She upset me for the same reason she had when I'd seen her in class rooms.

Although Ruby watched me closely, we ate in silence. I wondered if my attitude toward Carol was worthwhile. Why not go down there and invite her and her friends up for a drink or something? What difference did it make if she knew Ruby and I were shacking? She'd already found out, no doubt. I pushed back my plate and sighed meaningfully.

"More coffee?" Ruby asked.

"No, thanks. I'm going swimming, Carol or no Carol."

"That's the boy!" she said. "Who cares about her?"

That should've wised me up but it didn't. I gave time enough to finish eating, then went to my car and took out my belongings. By the time I came back Ruby was preparing to put on her suit.

I watched her with interest, and almost lost a decision to postpone swimming. As she dropped everything to the floor and began stepping into her suit, I evaluated her over and over again. She squirmed and twisted, working the stretchy material over her hips, finally slipping her arms under the straps. By the time her breasts were hidden, I'd stepped up to her, catching her by surprise. When we melted together she said,

"To get a suit to fit, you have to have them tight. Then they're hard to put on."

"Yes, but you're beautiful crawling into it! I almost want to do something else besides swim."

"It's up to you. Whatever you say."

"I know," and I released her. "Come on, let's go."

111

We walked to within three feet of Carol before she saw us.

"Well, well! How-do-you-do?" she said, sitting up.

"Hello, Carol," I said.

"What brings you this far down on the beach?" Ruby asked her.

"Better beach here," she said. "You know Tommy, Ruby. Tommy, this is Allan."

"Pleased to meet you," and the guy stuck out his mitt.

"Same here," I said, giving him a firm shake. "How's the water?"

"Don't know. Haven't been in yet," he said.

Hurriedly I left them and went into the surf. It wasn't that I was anxious to swim, either. Shortly after I'd dived into the water, Ruby came in. She reached to where I treaded water and, between mouthfuls of water, she said,

"Tommy's the guy who's the thickest with Carol."

"I'm not interested."

"Well, thought I'd tell you."

As soon as a large swell materialized, I caught it and rode it in. I went on then to a lonely spot and sprawled upon the sand. Like a shadow, Ruby joined me, trying to shake the water from her hair.

"Hey, you two!" Carol called. "Why don't you come over here?"

"More room over here," Ruby called back.

That was that for a while, and I flopped onto my stomach and began enjoying the sun beating down on my wet back.

"I thought those other kids were with Carol and Tommy," Ruby said. "But I guess they're not."

112

I mumbled, nothing audible, and turned my face so I could see Carol. She was playing in the sand, and Tommy was standing, like he might be contemplating a swim. He was very good-looking, not too large a guy, and he was cotton-blond with blue eyes. He was probably five-ten, plenty tall for Carol.

We whiled away most of the afternoon in like fashion, and strangely enough Carol and Tommy remained. Several times Ruby suggested that she invite them to the house for a drink, but I ruled it out. I was happy that they kept away from us.

On the dot of five, Carol came over to where Ruby and I lay. She put her foot on my back, pressed rather hard, then said,

"So long, unsociable. We're leaving now."

"Come back tomorrow," I suggested, rolling from under her foot and sitting up.

She seemed to ignore the invitation, and Ruby also sat up.

"You remember the guy I was telling you about, Allan?" Carol asked.

"Yes."

"Tommy's the one. You like him?"

"He's a good-looking hombre," I told her. "You two make a nice couple."

"You do for a fact, Carol," Ruby said.

"Yes," and Carol sighed tiredly. "Well, be seeing you two!"

I watched her walk away, slowly and somewhat dejectedly. In a way I was ashamed for not having been more sociable to her and her friend. I felt even worse about it when Ruby said,

"I feel like a fool for not inviting them up for a drink. But you came over here..."

113

"That's right. I didn't want a drink with them. Let's go back to the house."

No sooner had we entered when Ruby reminded me that she had made a date with Helen for that evening, but she'd break it if I wanted her to.

"Going out with some guys?" I asked.

"Oh, no!" she said, hurrying to confront me, putting her arms around me. "I won't go if you don't want me to."

I didn't want her to but I wouldn't admit it.

"You should go, since you promised," I told her.

"I won't be out very late. And when I get back. . ."

I pulled from her grasp, acutally suspecting that she and Helen were going out with men.

"What time do you have to go?" I asked.

"I'm to meet her at seven. Now, Allan, if you don't want me to go. . ."

"Go ahead. I wouldn't want you to disappoint Helen."

"All right. But no more. From now on, I'm going to save all the evenings for you."

"That's exactly what I don't want you to do," I said.

"Why?"

"I want you to feel free to do what you want to do."

"Because you want to do what you want to do?"

"Maybe." I said. "I'm going to get this wet suit off."

I let her think that over. But it didn't alter the fact that I'd become jealous of her—didn't really want her, yet didn't want anybody else to have her.

114

CHAPTER FIFTEEN

It wasn't going too well with me. Eight o'clock. Ruby had been gone an hour and already I was ready to get out of the beach house. And I likely would've had there not been a knock on the door. Who it was meant nothing to me. I didn't care and took my time about answering. When I opened the door there was Carol.

"Am I welcome?" she asked.

"Why not? Where's your shadow?"

"Tommy didn't especially need me tonight. Mother and Ruby had a couple of guys dated, so that left me home alone, which I don't like."

"Come on in," I said, boiling from an inner rage about Ruby's deception.

She stepped cautiously inside, glanced around, as if she suspected that somebody else might be there.

"Kick off your shoes and be comfortable," I suggested. "The old girl has some fire-water here. We can get on one."

"You seem in the right mood tonight!" she said, literally kicking off her pumps. "I'm surprised Ruby kept her date tonight. It even surprised me this morning when she called to tell us you and she had retired to the beach house."

"You're kidding!" I said, gaping widely. "She didn't call to tell you that."

"What makes you say so?"

"Because I asked her, and she said she didn't. Like I asked her if she and your mother were going with guys tonight, and she said no to that."

115

Carol tightened her lower lip and made an odd face.

"Well, Carol," she said to herself. "I guess you pulled another boner! Why can't I learn to keep my mouth shut?"

"Maybe you shouldn't, not in a case like this. The girl lied to me, Carol."

"Well," and she tilted her head to one side, made another face. "A lot of people like to tell a fib once in a while."

"Yeah," I agreed, burned up. "I guess they do at that."

Carol was dressed in yellow and she looked trim and neat. She walked uncertainly to a chair, spread her skirt, then sat very gracefully.

Quite abruptly I went into the kitchen. With little or no skill I mixed two drinks, giving her Seven Up, which was the only thing there besides a cola. I loaded both drinks, with the sole intention of stepping life up a bit. I hurried back, like maybe there was little time left to go somewhere.

"Thank you, dear Allan," she said. Then, after a taste, "Holy cow! What'd you do, empty the bottle in this drink?"

"Don't let it bother you. Drink it, it'll make hair grow on your chest!" I took a great swig of my drink, burning my throat.

"But I don't want any hair on my chest!" she protested, laughing. "What would I look like if I were as hairy as you?"

"I don't know. Right now, I don't know anything."

I sat down and Carol came over to me. She slipped her arm around my neck, squeezed some, then asked,

116

"Did my telling you about Ruby and Mother go-ing out make you feel badly?"

"No. It's none of my business what they do. Why should I care?"

"I don't know. I'd assumed Ruby had told you about it. The truth, I mean."

"I don't want Ruby to become a problem to me."

"She is going to become a problem if you aren't careful. You stick around with her long enough, and you'll feel you can't do without her. That's what happened to the guy who married her. He told me he couldn't leave her. And he didn't, either, until she stepped out on him so much."

Women knew what other women were doing, and I guessed then that all of them knew exactly what to do, how to hook a guy with their assets.

"I have a problem, Allan," she said, jiggling the ice in her glass.

"What kind of a problem?"

"A sex problem. I wouldn't tell anybody but you, not even Mother."

"A sex problem?" and I looked apprehensively at her.

"Yes. A doctor told me I should have an affair; said that not having had one was causing me a lot of my trouble."

I was supposed to believe that. I wanted to laugh aloud, still, it wasn't my nature to purposely hurt anybody. I acted indifferently to her statement, deciding to go along with the fib.

"I could go off some place where nobody knows me," she said. "But all sorts of things could happen if I did that. I could get a disease, maybe even pregnant."

"You could get pregnant in any case," I said.

"Why don't you step up this marriage deal, get that Tommy on the ball?"

"He's in law school. He wants to wait until after he's practiced for at least a year."

"What's wrong with you and him getting together that way?"

"Are you crazy?" she asked. "I couldn't afford to do anything with him. He'd think I was a regular whore!"

"Oh!" I then recalled that her mother had suffered from a similar difficulty when she was going with Jim Darwin. "I can't see anything wrong with doing something with the guy you intend to marry."

"I can!" she said. "God, I'd never live it down! He'd throw it in my face as long as I lived with him."

There I had it again. Women had more sex problems than men. I was too naive to understand what Carol's motive was in telling me her troubles. I'd become a big brother to her, and now we were discussing the woman's side of life.

"I didn't dare mention to Tommy that you and Ruby were sleeping together," she pursued. "If I had, he'd think *all* women sleep with men before they're married—except his mother and sisters, of course."

"Can't a guy tell if his wife's been with somebody?" I asked, assuming any dumb-bell could.

"My doctor told me there are outs to that problem."

"Oh?"

She'd been sipping the strong drink, and I'd been working on mine. She was rubbing my back now, and I could feel the warmth of her hand through my thin shirt.

118

"This drink is simply horrible, Allan! I think you're trying to get me drunk, so you can take advantage of me."

"Don't you want to be taken advantage of?" I asked. "Aren't you having that kind of problem?"

She got up, walked a few steps, then turned to stare down at me. For nearly a minute we exchanged glances, and she was peering at me over the rim of the glass, drinking some as she did so. Finally, she removed the glass from her lips.

"You really aren't a dummy, Allan," she said. "You're right. Why else was I telling you all that? I don't have anybody else to tell it to. You're just the kind of guy women pick on to confide in. I'm sort of ashamed now."

"You shouldn't be. Nobody'll ever know what you've told me."

"That's why I told you," she said. "I know you won't tell. Funny. When I came back from Rhode Island, Mother began telling me about you. What a wonderful boy she thought you were! Close-mouthed, she said. Strong, eager, honest, and had the greatest respect for women. She said all those things about you, Allan."

"Very nice," and there was a lump in my throat. I wished I weren't so sentimental.

"And as much as I figured you liked Mother, you left without telling her I'd invited and had you there. You see, that's why I know you won't tell."

She whirled and walked to the bay windows. Still sipping the drink, she gazed out, and she was standing in a relaxed manner, her feet and legs set apart. My pulse quickened and, for a moment, I fancied myself married to her, even allowed my mind to race back to our school days. I'd been afraid of her then, and now I was still afraid of her.

"You know," she said, facing me again, "everyone who knows me thinks I'm an easy mark for every lame-brain I go with. I think Mother even thinks I lost my virtue several years ago. Do I care? Maybe. But I don't really believe I do. No matter how moral you try to be, somebody's trying to break you down, ruin your reputation, by gossiping and pointing."

"Don't get bitter," I warned.

"Bitter? Maybe I am bitter. Do you remember when I used to smoke?"

"Yes."

"I don't smoke any more, had you noticed?"

"No, I hadn't."

"You see? People never notice good things you do, nor bad things you *don't* do."

I had no comment. I disagreed silently with her, as she had voiced good things she thought about me, which indicated that my virtues had been observed. I was ready for another drink and I said,

"Drink up!"

"I don't want another drink here," she said. "I'm not comfortable in Ruby's house."

"Neither am I. But right now I have no choice."

"You have. We have my house to go to."

"All right," I agreed readily. "I don't want to be here when Ruby comes back."

"I wouldn't be either, if I were you. You're too nice a guy to be lied to like that."

"Thanks, Carol. I'll wash the glasses and we'll be off. I'll drive behind you, and ditch my car on some side street."

"Why do you have to ditch your car?"

"So Ruby won't see it, in case we're still there when they get through with their fun."

"What burns me up is that she makes it a point to let me know she's shacking with you."

"It riles me, too. I'll be ready in a jiffy."

On our way to Carol's, my thoughts were all mingled as I drove behind her. Somehow I knew I wasn't really escaping from Ruby by leaving her house. I felt her everywhere. Her frantic, sensual breathing still seemed to flow into my ears. As I contemplated a fling with Carol, I told myself that it'd be only to help her. Like Helen had said, I'd have done Ruby a favor, had I taken advantage of her drunkenness.

As planned, I drove to a side street and parked my car. When I reached the house, Carol was waiting for me. We went in and she was careful to limit the light to two dim floor lamps.

"You don't have to worry now," she told me. "Mother and Ruby won't come back until late in the morning, and maybe not all night."

It was like she was cutting and drying what was to take place, and I figured myself pretty smart for thinking I'd guessed. At the same time something in my stomach turned over nauseously when I thought of Ruby staying out so late. Carol came to me and pressed her body closely against me.

"Allan, I'm going to be terribly embarrassed, even with all the lights out. Promise me you'll understand—remember that I don't intend being an awful person—that I *must* do something about myself."

We'd begun to embrace now, and I kissed Carol casually. Her reciprocation was matter-of-fact,

121

only she was trying to control an inner, burning desire, somewhat reluctant to release nature's door to her plight.

"I've stood this, Allan, even back as far as the night I asked you to kiss me. I didn't know very much about it then, and I guess you didn't either. If I try to change my mind, don't let me. If I become unruly, or I tell you to stop, just ignore me. I promise I won't be angry when it's over."

Her glibness had given rise to a new desire in me, and she was becoming a swelling wedge between Ruby's hold on me. The mind was fickle, I knew, and so was the body, I decided. But where would it all end? Would the intimacy with Carol tear me from Ruby, only to weld me to Carol?

"We'd better go to my room for the very start," she suggested. "If you want to drink, I'll fix something. But since this whole idea is so insane, perhaps we'd best be as sane and sober as possible."

"You're right," I vaguely heard myself say.

Then she was holding my hand, sort of leading me from the front room where the basic conspiracy had begun. Prior to my affair with Ruby this might have been too breath-taking for me to bear with such fortitude. But since such an experience was behind me and Carol apparently was aware of her own problem, I went along without hesitation.

Some light filtered into the room when we entered, enough to give a general idea where the furniture was placed. She closed the bedroom door, plunging us into darkness. She found my hand and squeezed it with all her strength.

How do you tell of an experience like this?

122

Where darkness prevails, both for mind and body? It would be hard to explain my chagrin when I learned that she had told the truth; that sex with her had existed only in her mind.

I disliked myself for having doubted her. My respect for Ruby decreased, because she had made statements which caused me to prejudge Carol. Dozens of things ran passion a close race while the darkness shielded us from our own shame. I lost track of time as though it were mingled with other factors which no longer interested me. My sole interest was there in that room. A frightened girl to whom for so many years ago I'd become attracted.

The road had been long and hard, unlike a planned pleasure trip that an affair of this sort should be. Carol cried, at the same time holding onto me as if I was her last hope to avoid plunging over the cliff—to death. Behind it all, I felt she had no real reason to fear life, nor what had happened between us. Yet, I refused to deny her any fraction of the right to her own obsessions.

"Carol." I said softly. "Please don't cry any more."

"I can't help it."

"Are you sorry?"

"No, no!" and she held me tighter. "It's just that...I don't know...maybe I shouldn't have... just hold me!"

"You helped *me*, Carol," I whispered. "Do you understand."

"Yes, Allan. I'm glad. Don't give me up because I'm such a cry baby."

I stroked her back, kissed her ear, only two of a hundred things I wanted to do. And I hoped with

123

all sincerity that Carol would be my last girl.

CHAPTER SIXTEEN

Neither Carol nor I ever knew if Helen had caught us together in the room. She had gone the following morning before we'd dared show ourselves. Anyhow, if Helen had known, there was no immediate mention of it to Carol. That same morning, shortly after a cup of coffee with Carol, I drove back to Redlands.

Though I tried hard to conceal it, my unhappiness was quite obvious to people I knew and saw in the inland city. I hadn't wanted to go back to Ruby's because the affair with Carol had torn me free from the older girl. No doubt about it, I was involved in a bad situation. I was in a stew pot over Carol. It was true that she'd asked me, had practically begged me, to stay on in Venice. But in the face of that suggestion stood both Tommy and Ruby.

Job-wise I'd been lucky during the week I'd been back. A friend recommended me for a sales position in an appliance store and I was accepted. On the strength of this I rented a small apartment on Sixth Street, an upstairs affair, with kitchen and bath. It seemed so shabby compared to Ruby's house, her beach place, and the home in which Carol lived.

But with the help of the landlady and a few dollars spent for curtains and a table cloth, it didn't look too bad. Some older man had lived there for several years, and hadn't cared how the place looked. Perhaps I might've felt the same

124

way if Carol hadn't promised to come to Redlands to see me.

I dropped Carol a note Wednesday, telling her I'd moved. The rest of the week passed and I neither saw nor heard from her. But Monday evening when I came from work Ruby was parked, waiting for me. I'd spotted the car half a block away and figured she'd seen me through her rear view mirror before I parked behind her.

By the time I was out of my car, Ruby was waiting on the sidewalk for me. She didn't appear angry; instead there was a challenging grin on her face.

"Hello, Allan."

"Hello," I said. "What brings you in this direction?"

"I happened to see your letter to Carol, and I just decided to pay *you* a visit."

"Was she that proud of my letter? Showing it around to everybody?"

"She didn't show it. Helen showed it to me. I hope you don't mind my stopping by."

"I don't mind, Ruby," I said. "Do you want to come upstairs? My dump isn't anything like where you live."

"That doesn't matter," she said. "I'd like to go up. I took the liberty of introducing myself to your landlady—as your sister."

"You didn't, Ruby!" and I glanced at the house, hoping we hadn't been overheard.

"Don't worry," she said. "Your landlady's gone to do some marketing. And besides, she asked me point-blank if I was your sister—said we looked alike. So I told her yes."

"Come on," I said.

She followed me, her high heels echoing through the place like somebody driving spikes in a crosstie. Once inside she sat on the day bed and stretched her legs. I hung up my coat and took off my tie. Despite all my resolutions that I wanted to keep away from her, she was tempting as hell.

"Funny the way you left, Allan," she ventured casually.

"Let's not talk about the past," I said. "A lot of things in this world are funny. How long are you staying in town?"

"I don't know. I don't have any special time to get back. You know the way I live."

"Yeah. I know the way you live. But I live a different way. I have to work, and I just got a new job, and it's going to be tough for a few weeks."

"You don't *have* to work," she said. "You were in a good position—before you left me."

"That's the past again," I reminded her. "If you stay longer than tonight, you'll have to find your own fun all day tomorrow."

"That's okay. I don't mind," and she kicked off her shoes. "I read in your letter to Carol that you're selling washing machines and stoves."

"That's true." And I added happily, "I sold two washing machines today."

"Either a lot of dirty people here, or a lot of clean ones," was her remark. "I don't suppose you have anything around to drink?"

"No. And I don't have a refrigerator."

"I never did understand men," she said. "But *you* take the cake! You leave practically everything for absolutely *nothing*."

126

"I do have a stove, and I can make coffee. Would you like some?"

"No. But if you have any water, I'd go for that —among other things—like a kiss...something to show me you aren't too put out about my coming."

I ignored the kiss part and went to the ice-box and commenced chipping some ice to put in her water. Soon she was there, her arms around my waist, and she tightened her grasp. I walked to the sink and she followed me, still holding on.

"Here's your water," and I broke loose and faced her.

"Thank you! I hate to drink this stuff, but I'm thirsty as hell. It's too hot over here."

"I don't mind it," I said.

She drank the water, making an unpleasant face, then she handed back the glass. I put it down and went back to my front room. As she followed she said,

"Why don't you want to live on the beach? Everything's nicer there."

"You mean live with you?"

"You could do a lot worse, and from the looks of things, you won't be happy here."

I sat down and she followed suit. She seemed very nervous when she dug out a cigarette and lit it. Perhaps it was unfair but I began comparing her with Carol. The latter might be as passionate as Ruby, yet she was in full control, trying to refrain from promiscuity. There was no real sense in making such an analogy and I brushed it from my mind.

"Some people can be very happy in the oddest places," I reminded her. "Maybe a lot of our

127

happiness should come from within. You aren't happy, else you wouldn't be *here.*"

"I'll have to give you credit," she said. "You are right. You might tell me, though, why you skipped out like you did. Of course, you did that with Helen."

"There was a difference," I said. "But in either case, I didn't belong."

"That's your opinion and you're entitled to it. What will our eating schedule be?"

"I'll take you out for dinner. I do very little eating here."

"I feel hot and sticky, may I take a bath?"

"Certainly."

"Would you help me bring my things up?"

"Your *things*?"

"Yes, silly. I didn't come for just a few minutes' visit."

"Sure. We'll bring them up. I guess if you convinced the landlady that you're my sister, she won't think anything about it."

"She's convinced, don't you worry about that. As a matter of fact, she said she had a folding-bed we could bring up here. You know, she probably thinks a brother and sister shouldn't sleep together, especially on such a small bed."

I began hoping, as I looked sideways at her, that if Carol ever decided to come, she wouldn't tell the landlady the same story.

"We'll go down after your clothes," I told her.

Down the stairs and back up again Ruby yaked. Her back had been bothering her, and she'd discovered some kind of female trouble. She wished she were as healthy as Carol, who, she said, was still running rampant with every guy she could

128

find, and who would very likely end up pregnant in no time at all. This burned me some and I turned on her and said:

"Cut that crap, will you?"

"Allan! Imagine you saying a word like that!"

"The word I used isn't nearly as bad as your catty accusations. Let up on the girl, and clean around your own back door."

She put her hand to her face like I'd slapped her, and her eyes grew very large.

"If you aren't the one!" she blasted. "I thought you were a guy who respected all women."

"I do when they deserve respect. I happen to know that a lot of things you say about Carol is baloney. And she's Helen's daughter, and you're supposed to be Helen's friend."

"All right!" she said, stamping her foot. "You told me what I wanted to know. You're so stuck on Carol you don't know what to do!"

"I won't deny that, nor will I admit it. But I'm going to have proof she's a whore before I call her one. And I think you should have proof first, too."

"I guess you think I'm one?" she flared.

"I didn't say you were. But if the shoe fits, wear it."

She folded her arms across her breasts and turned her back to me. For nearly five minutes she stared out the window, sighing spasmodically —her temper outwardly showing. Then she whirled around and came toward me.

"You can think what you want about Carol," she said. "And you can go nuts over her if you like. But you'll never get her. You don't have the class she's looking for. And you don't have the money. Why, Allan, who do you think you are? She has some of the best running after her."

"Do me a favor, will you?" I asked.

"Sure. I'm just the type of sucker who'd do almost anybody a favor. Shoot!"

"Why don't you go back to Venice? I think you're too far out of your class, too."

"Allan!" she flung her arms around me. "I'm your type, don't you see that? Can't you see that we're suited for each other?"

It was the first time I'd ever pushed a woman away from me. At that moment I didn't want her touching me. She stood back, gaping at me, and I was sorry I'd done it.

"I'd have done anything for you, Allan. More than any woman would have. Like I offered you a home, with anything you needed. So you give me a shove. You stick up for Carol and run me down."

"Get off it!" I yelled, turning away from her. "You're all hot and bothered. Go douse yourself in a tub of cold water. I don't want to argue with you any more."

Suddenly she was on my back, as it were, hugging me from behind. Her hands were clasped against my stomach and I covered them with my own hands. I couldn't stay angry at her. In spite of all her screwball ways she was real and human. And she was lonely. And like the way she had to live it was rough.

"It's okay, Ruby," I said, patting her hands now. "Go take your bath and we'll go snatch a bite."

"You're making a better woman out of me, Allan," she said. "I'm glad you told me off."

The storm had abated and everything was fine.

130

Ruby took out her clean lingerie, disrobed, and for several minutes pranced about, remarking how nice it was to be free of warm clothes. That was all right, I guessed, but her vibrant nudity upset me and the warm day began to affect me.

Before surrendering to a tub of water, she suggested that I take a bath—to cool me off—and to save time, the two of us should bathe together. It seemed logical enough and I agreed. But you don't take a bath with a girl like Ruby to save time; even if you're the most naive man alive. It should've appeared that my stupidity got me a break but she came closer to getting her way than I did.

The town was lighted and it was late when we went to eat. In a smaller restaurant we selected an empty booth toward the rear. Soon after the waitress had taken our orders, Ruby turned to me.

"There was something I intended telling you, Allan."

"What?" I asked.

"About Carol...and please don't pounce on me. I'll tell you real fast, before you have a chance to blow up. Carol told her mother last night that she's getting married. And guess who to?"

"I haven't the slightest idea." I lied.

"Tommy. Apparently they'd decided a long time ago to take the plunge, but were holding back because he wanted to finish school. Something new came up and they changed their minds, so Carol tells her mother for the first time that it's serious with him."

Immediately I took the blame. Had it not been for the affair, she wouldn't have made the decision. I ached inside, like when you grieve because some loved one's going away. No wonder Carol hadn't come. I tried my best to act nonchalant in Ruby's presence, but I knew my let-down attitude betrayed me.

CHAPTER SEVENTEEN

Ruby was waiting for me at the door, and I was paying the check when somebody took a strong grip around my arm. I turned quickly and faced Ken.

"Hello, Allan!" he said eagerly.

"What are you doing here?" I was happy to see him.

"I've been looking for you," he revealed. "I went to where you used to live and they didn't know where you'd gone."

"Ruby," I said. "Come over here and meet a friend."

I introduced them and we stood chatting, and I suppose the cashier thought we were in no hurry. Anyhow, Ken's job in Long Beach hadn't materialized and, since I'd been to his house to see him, he'd decided to visit me. He'd been eating at the counter and was getting ready to go back to Venice.

Finally, when the bill was paid, we cleared out and rode back to my dump. On the way Ruby gave Ken considerable notice, and, once we were inside the apartment she made her interest more obvious. Ken was embarrassed, and he blushed. Maybe I was jealous of Ruby; or perhaps she was crumming me up with a friend and it was bothering me. It didn't matter too much, except that Ken,

132

despite his embarrassment, seemed interested in her.

Ruby acted very decently. She sat properly, kept her skirt well over her knees and didn't cross her legs too many times. She kept in our conversation, managing to tell Ken where she lived, and dig out of him where he lived. It was all very subtle, like banging somebody over the head with a sledge.

Ken persisted in taking the midnight bus back to Venice, so I excused myself to Ruby, making it clear to her that I wanted to take him to the station alone. Once we were in the car, rolling, Ken asked,

"She your steady?"

"No. I don't have a steady. Nice kid, though," I made the mistake of saying.

"I saw that other girl one time," he said. "You know, the one you used to like?"

"Oh, yes," I said, as if I'd almost forgotten her. "Where'd you see her?"

"In a theater in Ocean Park. She's sure a good-looking kitten."

"I guess. Tell me, Ken do you go with anybody?"

"Nobody special."

He skimmed over some of his experiences, but he was so close-mouthed you couldn't get head or tail of what he was talking about. He'd become a handsome guy and he had a winning personality. It wasn't hard to see why Ruby'd get excited about him.

It seemed no time at all that I was back to the apartment. During my absence the landlady had helped Ruby carry up the folding bed, and it was

133

there, in the front room, all made up and ready to sleep on.

Ruby was quiet and docile and she was wrapped in a filmy kimona. I was tempted to quiz her about Ken, to see if she'd discuss the attention she'd given him, but somehow I wasn't bothered hardly enough to care. Good or bad, my thoughts were on Carol and her marriage to Tommy.

"Would you mind too much if I went back to-morrow?" Ruby asked me.

"Of course not."

"Well, you'll be working, and I don't know what I'd do with myself all day."

That was Ruby. She'd have to have a man she could support, one she could keep with her through most of the hours of the day. Between times she could have her extra flings, constantly seeking variety, but holding onto at least one as assurance that she'd never be completely alone.

Though two beds were available, Ruby crowded in with me but we found no need for one another. She fell asleep sooner than I, but for more than an hour I lay awake before I finally slept.

It was no problem to wake Ruby. We hurried about, getting her things in order and packing her suitcases in her car. She drove behind me to the restaurant where we'd eaten the night before. It was more evident than ever that she'd given me up, made a decision that I wasn't for her. We ate in silence.

I'd put a tip on the table and picked up the check when she said,

"I feel sorry for you, Allan."

"Why?"

134

"Because you're so crazy about Carol and she doesn't give a damn for you. Why do you think I'm leaving this morning?"

"I really haven't any idea," I lied. "I guess I was going by what you said last night."

"No, Allan. That wasn't really it. To you, I'd never be anyone but someone to chase—just another dame."

"Shall we go?" I asked her.

"Sure. You have to go to work. Too bad it couldn't have been the other way."

I answered her with a sigh as I stepped out of the booth. From there to her car short stabs dug at my stomach, the kind you feel when you aren't happy about what's happening. I stood by her car, my elbows on the window ledge, waiting for her to say something.

"How much do you really like Carol?" she asked.

"Too damn much," I admitted. "I guess I've always liked her that much."

"Too bad, Well, goodbye, Allan."

"So long."

Then she was gone and I watched the car until it turned a corner. There was one thing I was sure of: Ruby was out of my life.

The past possessed me all that day. And when I returned to the apartment that evening, I found a letter from Carol. She expressed regret for our affair, and after revealing the facts to Tommy, he had realized her sexual need, therefore had agreed that they should get married. To her, I was still one of the swellest guys in the world, she wrote.

A lot of good compliments had ever done me, I told myself as I folded her letter. I figured this

135

Tommy must be quite a guy himself, knowing she had been with me and still wanting to marry her. But you really never like a guy who's going to marry the girl you think you love. And ordinarily you'd figure Tommy was a sucker for marrying a girl you'd had. But I had a different answer. I was the prize sucker.

Days passed by, none of which brought anything of consequence. A few interesting letters came from Ken, and he was honest enough to admit that Ruby had glided up to his house one evening, and they were getting on quite cozily together. I wasn't much for praying but I said at least one prayer; asking that Ken be spared from any hurt which might affect his life in later years.

I took to the appliance business more eagerly than ever, and had chalked up some pretty swift strides in salesmanship. Two months later the store was sold to a Los Angeles firm and some personnel was sent to Redlands. A representative from a major appliance company, with whom I'd become friendly, recommended me to the new owners and, due to my good record, I was transferred to one of their larger stores in Los Angeles, a move bringing me to within fifteen miles of the beach, incentive enough to spend time there, had I wanted to. But for some strange reason I refused to yield to my desires, and I stopped corresponding with Ken. When you live in Los Angeles, it rarely happens that you accidentally run into someone you know. And since I didn't care to take that chance, I felt as safe as I needed to be.

My safety was short lived. The appliance firm opened another store, this time in Ocean Park. It was my big break. With only four months with the new company, I was promoted to store manager, and my duties there began about the middle of January. During the first two weeks it was pretty rough. Running the show was very different from just playing a role on the stage, and my lack of business experience began to show.

My tenure at the store might have come to an early end had it not been for a woman with whom I'd had previous business dealings. The gloomy afternoon she walked into the store could have been one of the very worst days of my life. I heard her demand to see the manager and I went hurriedly toward her, dreading a similar hassle I'd had once before with her.

"Hello, Mr. West!" she greeted.

"Good to see you again, Mrs. Strom," I said. "Isn't this terrible weather we're having?"

"It is. And according to the weather man, we'll have more. I have some good news for you, Mr. West. I've decided to furnish my new apartment buildings with your appliances."

This was a windfall! How many stoves and refrigerators was she going to use, I asked myself? My enthusiasm and smile obviously expressed my appreciation.

"I might remind you," she offered, "that the reason I came back here was because you were the nicest of all the store managers I talked to."

I never did recall our exact conversation that day, but I learned that we were going to get an unusually large order. The dismal January day turned into one of the brightest.

Business picked up from then on, and through February, March, April and May, the store did well

137

enough so that I'd proved my capability as a store manager. My salary had grown with the business, and I thought I was commencing a new life when I rented a beach house large enough for a normal-sized family. It was located within a block from where Carol and Helen had lived when I'd first met them, and about a mile north of Ruby's beach house.

Being so close to them, I often wondered about them; how Ken and Ruby came out and, more than all, how Carol and Tommy were getting along. As much as I wanted to know, and as lonesome as I'd sometimes get, I made no effort to see any of them. Some evenings I'd walk on the beach. I'd forgotten exactly which house was Ruby's. Perhaps I passed it many times, for my strolls were often quite distant. Something about the roaring surf and the soft sand soothed my loneliness, and I felt that my prosperity had finally given me a victory over the strife I'd once known.

Now it was July and I was winning another great battle over a part of my past. I'd met a young woman, a customer from the store, and we'd made a date and were going out. It was a warm evening and I had an hour to kill. I looked out at the rolling surf and decided to take a quick dip before dressing, and the beach there was deserted. Usually around six the crowds were gone, so I slipped into my trunks and padded out onto the sand, and waded into the water.

I'd scarcely worked my way beyond the surf when a group of laughing people descended on the beach, having come from between my house and the neighboring one. The first person my eyes spotted was Ken. Beside him, holding firmly to his arm, was Ruby. While I treaded water, I saw Helen, who held onto the arm of a portly appearing gentleman. There were half a dozen others I'd never seen before. All of them were clad in swimming attire, and some of them carried picnic baskets.

I saw that some of them were watching me, but all they could see was my head. Ken was looking my way, and had he recognized me, he'd have given some sign. I could hear them talking and laughing, a jolly bunch; and two of the women spread blankets over the sand.

I might not have given them another thought, for I was planning to swim some distance north before getting out of the water. But I heard a feminine voice call out,

"Where's Carol?"

I looked again, this time seeing Carol coming toward the others.

"She's coming." I recognized Helen's voice. "I wonder if that guy's drowning out there?"

Everybody looked at my head bobbing up and, despite the strong, setting sun reflecting into his eyes, Ken recognized me.

"Hey! That's Allan! Hey, Allan!" and his voice sounded like it used to when we were kids.

I stuck one hand up to wave and saw that Carol had stopped, more than twenty feet from where the bunch stood. My heart was pounding as if it might escape and race across the ocean.

Ken dashed away from them and ran as far as possible through the surf, then dived into a breaker and swam to me. We grasped hands, splashing water.

"Where in the hell have you been all this

139

time?'' he asked.

"Around," I said.

"Come on out and have a picnic with us."

"Thanks. I have a date."

"Come on," he said, "let's ride one in like we used to!"

I nodded and we moved surf-ward until a giant swell came. Both of us raced ahead of it and our timing was perfect. Almost instantly we picked ourselves off the sand and walked to where the others waited.

CHAPTER EIGHTEEN

Helen kissed me. Ruby kissed me. Ken shook hell out of my hand and slapped my shoulder almost raw. They introduced me to the others, but all this time Carol hadn't moved from where she'd stopped when Ken recognized me in the water. Finally I tore loose and went to her. She didn't smile, and I wasn't sure that she was even looking at me.

"Carol," I said, "you look great! Married life must really be agreeing with you."

"Thank you," she managed to say. "It's nice to see you again."

"Hey, you two!" Ruby yelled. "Come on, we're starving."

Carol shook her head, as though trying to dispel a trance.

"Will you picnic with us?" she asked.

"Thanks," I said. "But I have a dinner date."

"Well," and she smiled sickly, "maybe you

have time to visit with us?"

"I have a few minutes."

The group settled and it was necessary for me to beg off half a dozen times before they stopped insisting that I eat with them. Nibbling at a sandwich in her left hand, I noticed that Carol didn't wear her rings. Tommy wasn't there, and she was without an escort.

Helen, Ruby and Ken were firing questions at me, boring their friends. They wanted to know what I was doing and where I worked, and their faces were like masks when I admitted that for nearly a year I'd been rather close to them. When my phone began ringing, I excused myself and rushed to answer it.

It was my date. Some unexpected company had dropped in and she asked me to spend the evening at her house. No, I told her, we'd have a date some other time. I returned to the crowd, gave them the news, and they seemed delighted that I'd be with them.

Ken wore no scars from any possible difficulty with Ruby, which pleased me greatly. Helen was engaged to the man with her, but nobody mentioned Carol. Anxiety tore at me, and it was obvious from the way I felt that I shouldn't have run into Carol. There *were* some sweeping glances between my old friends when Ken mentioned that he'd tried so hard to locate me.

I learned that there was another member of the group still in one of the cars when Helen said,

"Ken, why don't you see if Gertrude hasn't changed her mind about eating something. This potato salad is absolutely delicious."

141

"I'll go, Mother," Carol suggested. "I imagine Loren's through eating anyhow."

Carol rose, and as she walked up the sandy incline, I was tempted to follow her, regardless of what anyone might think. I would have, had Helen not spoken to me.

"I take it you're not married yet, Allan?"

"No."

"Engaged?"

"No."

"That's funny," she said. "Carol didn't get married, either."

Again Helen, Ruby and Ken looked at one another, but nothing was said.

The man with Helen, as well as the other strangers, turned quizzical eyes upon me. Then he asked,

"Could this be the young man you've spoken so often about, Helen?"

"That's our boy," Helen said.

I began to seethe with resentment. Helen smiled.

"Nobody's been talking harshly about you, Allan," she went on.

"I hope not," I said, looking at Ken for any enlightenment.

"You're just one of those guys who doesn't give people a chance to say bad things about." Helen added, "But I'm afraid you're in for a big surprise, and I hope it doesn't throw you."

If ever I trembled in my life I was doing so then. Ken's eyes told me nothing, and his face had gone chalky. I followed his gaze. Carol was coming back, walking beside a middle-aged woman

142

who carried a baby in her arms.

They reached us and stopped. Carol looked at me, just as I was getting to my feet.

"Come over here," Carol said, her voice a little husky.

I went, conscious that everyone was watching my reaction. I looked at the baby in the woman's arms, and already I'd guessed the answer.

"She's your daughter, Allan," Carol said. "If you look closely enough, you'll see she resembles you, too."

I glanced only a moment at the tiny face and bald head. My stupid mind was in chaos and when I looked again at Carol she was crying. I was glad, and I was sad, all at once. Then I felt an arm around me, and I turned to see it was Helen.

"Go, Allan," she said to me. "You and Carol walk down the beach a ways. I know this is a terrible shock to you, but you aren't obligated in the least. Carol, straighten up."

Helen sort of turned both of us around and gently gave us a little push. We walked, and Carol's head was down, her body shaking convulsively from uncontrollable sobbing. I wanted to crush her in my arms but I was afraid that wasn't what she wanted. No heel ever felt more like a heel than I did.

We continued to walk, neither of us looking back, and I waited for her to call a halt and confront me with a hysterical outburst. She was so strangely different from the old days that it frightened hell out of me.

We probably walked half a mile. Every time I'd glance at her, it was the same; she held a hanky against her nose and she stared at the sand.

"Carol!" I said, halting. "This is far enough."

"Yes, Allan," and she stopped there, digging her toe into the sand. "I guess it's too late to tell you that I was such a fool—and that I loved you when all this happened."

"It's never too late for anything," I said, and I drew her closely to me. "What am I supposed to do? How am I supposed to act? You'll have to realize this is a hell of a shock to me!"

She withdrew her head from my chest and looked up at me through swollen eyes.

"Allan, you'll have to act the way you feel. If you want me and Loren we're yours. If you don't want us....."

I interrupted her.

"What do *you* want, Carol?"

"I want you to take us. My love for you has grown out of proportion, and if you don't love me, maybe you would later."

"That's a laugh!" I said, squeezing her tightly to me. "I hope I never love you any more than I do now."

"Allan!" she said, trying to get closer to me. "God sent you back to us. I know He did. He answered my prayers."

Maybe she was right. I didn't know and I didn't care who'd sent me back. All I cared about then was that I had Carol, what I'd always wanted since my school days. And what was more, back in Gertrude's arms I had something else, another girl, who'd be every bit as dear to me as Carol was.

Maybe to other people we looked mismatched,

like we were wrong for each other—petite Carol and me, an overgrown lug. But we didn't care. We were right for each other.

Later, when we returned to the party, the picnic was in full swing. The others looked at us... and I could tell from their expressions that they were sure we'd settled both our past and future together.

JURY VOTES FOR FABIAN AND SABER BOOKS

In April, 1958 the Government charged that *eleven books published by FABIAN and SABER BOOKS went substantially beyond contemporary community standards and appealed to the prurient interests of an average normal person. Before trial, the Government dismissed its case as to eight of the books and the case went to the jury as to the remaining three. After a three week trial, and after considering the case for some sixteen hours, the jury acquitted as to the book *Rambling Maids* and voted nine to three in favor of *The Strange Three* and *Turbulent Daughters*.

We are, of course, pleased with the outcome since we always felt that our books were within contemporary community standards. We would appreciate hearing from you advising us what you think of our books. We are particularly anxious to know if in your opinion any of our books deal too intimately with sex and whether you believe that they should be available to the average, normal person. Please address your communications to:

FABIAN BOOKS, LTD.
2919 East Belmont Avenue
Fresno 1, California

*The eight titles dropped in the original Government charge are:
FABIAN: *Rene, Black Night, Stairways To Sin, Dark Quarters, Tainted Wife, Violent Surrender, Taxi Dancers.*
SABER: *Karla.*

FABIAN BOOKS IN PRINT

Z-102	*SATAN'S HARVEST*	Sanford Aday
Z-103	*THE LADY WAS A MAN*	Mark Shane
Z-107	*RENE*	Kip Madigan
Z-109	*A ROAD DIVIDED*	Reese Hayes
Z-112	*THE BLACK NIGHT*	Betty Short
Z-113	*MY BED HAS ECHOES*	Sydney Omarr
Z-114	*STAIRWAYS TO SIN*	Kip Madigan
Z-116	*THE RAMBLING MAIDS*	Betty Short
Z-117	*THE DARK QUARTERS*	Stella Hampton
Z-118	*TAINTED WIFE*	Willi Peters
Z-119	*VIOLENT SURRENDER*	Cherri Southern
Z-120	*TAXI DANCERS*	Eve Linkletter
Z-121	*PUSH-OVER*	Lora Sela
Z-122	*HIGH PILLOW*	Betty Short
Z-123	*BEACH MAVERICK*	Floyd Haynes
Z-124	*THE GAY ONES*	Eve Linkletter
Z-125	*MAN IS A SEXUAL BEING*	W. de Ortega Maxey
Z-126	*NOR FEARS OF HELL*	William Bennett
Z-127	*IMPOSED REBELLION*	James Williams
Z-128	*OUR FLESH WAS CHEAP*	Eve Linkletter
Z-130	*TOMORROW'S LIGHT*	Dorothy Mencer
Z-131	*PASSIONATE LOVIE*	Dolores Dee
Z-133	*ROSE OF SHARON*	Lee Bradley
Z-134	*WITCH FINDER*	Ralph Brandon
Z-135	*NEVER TO BELONG*	James Williams

UNITED STATES SUPREME COURT
PROTECTS BOOKSELLERS

WASHINGTON, D. C.

On December 14, 1959, in a far-reaching decision, the United States Supreme Court ruled unconstitutional a Los Angeles ordinance under which a bookstore owner was convicted of having an "obscene" book in his place of business. The bookseller, through his attorney, argued that the law was so broad that innocent persons and constitutionally protected books were endangered under it. The City Attorney for Los Angeles contended that unless the City was free to dispense with the requirements of knowledge "regulation of the distribution of 'obscene' books will be ineffective." Justice Brennan, speaking for himself and Justices Warren, Whitaker, Stewart and Clark, rejected the City's argument, saying:

"By dispensing with the requirement of knowledge the ordinance tends to impose a severe limitation on the public's access to constitutionally protected materials."

In the main opinion, Justice Brennan emphasized that freedom of speech and press were fundamental rights which no arm of government could invade without offending the Constitution.

"Free publication and dissemination of books and other forms of the printed word" have always been jealously guarded by the courts, the Justice said. "A retail bookseller plays a most significant role in the distribution of books", he said, and it makes no difference "that the dissemination takes place under commerical auspices."

Justice Brennan observed that in the free speech area a law which may be applied to protected speech must fall because it threatens with criminal prosecution those who would exercise their rights of free expression. Moreover,

Justice Brennan continued: "This Court has intimated that stricter standards of permissible statutory vagueness may be applied to a statute having a potentially inhibiting effect of speech; a man may the less be required to act at his peril here, because the free dissemination of ideas may be the looser."

GOVERNMENT CANNOT RESTRICT DISTRIBUTION OF BOOKS

"We have held that obscene speech and writings are not protected by the constitutional guarantees of freedom of speech and the press. The ordinance here in question, to be sure, only imposes criminal sanctions on a bookseller if there in fact is to be found in his shop an obscene book. But our holding in Roth does not recognize any state power to restrict the dissemination of books which are not obscene; and we think this ordinance's strict liability feature would tend seriously to have that effect, by penalizing booksellers, even though they had not the slightest notice of the character of the books they sold."

THE ORDINANCE IMPOSES SEVERE LIMITATIONS ON FREE SPEECH

"By dispensing with any requirement of knowledge of the contents of the book on the part of the seller, the ordinance tends to impose a severe limitation on the public's access to constitutionally protected matter. For if the bookseller is criminally liable without knowledge of the contents, and the ordinance fulfills its purpose, he will tend to restrict the books he sells to those he has inspected; and thus the State will have imposed a restriction upon the distribution of constitutionally protected as well as obscene literature. It has been well observed of a statute construed as dispensing with any requirement of scienter that: 'Every bookseller would be placed under an obligation to make himself aware of the contents of every book in his shop. It would be altogether unreasonable to demand so near an approach to omniscience.' And the bookseller's burden would become the public's burden, for by restricting him the public's access to reading matter would be restricted. If the contents of bookshops and periodical stands were restricted to material of which their proprietors had made an inspection, they might be depleted indeed. The bookseller's limitation in the amount of reading material with which he could familiarize himself, and his timidity in the face of his absolute criminal liability, thus would tend to restrict the public's access to forms of the printed word which the State could not constitutionally suppress directly. The bookseller's self-censorship compelled by the State, would be a censorship affecting the whole public, hardly less virulent for being privately administered. Through it, the distribution of all books, both obscene and not obscene, would be imposed."

FEDERAL AND STATE INTRUSION MUST BE CONTROLLED

"The fundamental freedoms of speech and press have contributed greatly to the development and well-being of our free society and are indispensable to its continued growth. Ceaseless vigilance is the watchword to prevent their erosion by Congress or by the States. The door barring federal and state intrusion into this area cannot be left ajar; it must be kept tightly closed and opened only the slightest crack necessary to prevent encroachment upon more important interests. This ordinance opens that door too far. The existence of the State's power to prevent the distribution of obscene matter does not mean that there can be no constitutional barrier to any form of practical exercise of that power. It is plain to us that the ordinance in question, though aimed at obscene matter has such a tendency to inhibit constitutionally protected expression that it cannot stand under the Constitution."

JUSTICE BLACK AGAINST ALL OBSCENITY LAWS

Justice Black agreed that the ordinance was unconstitutional but did not think the Court went far enough. As he saw it "prison sentences for possession of 'obscene' books will seriously burden freedom of the press whether punishment is imposed with or without knowledge of obscenity."

Justice Black continued: "Certainly the First Amendment's language leaves no room for inference that abridgments of speech and press can be made just because they are slight. That Amendment provides, in simple words, that 'Congress shall make no law...abridging the freedom of speech, or of the press.' I read 'no law abriding' to mean NO LAW ABRIDGING. The First Amendment, which is the supreme law of the land, has thus fixed its own value on freedom of speech and press by putting these freedoms wholly 'beyond the reach' of federal power to abridge. No other provision of the Constitution porports to dilute the scope of these unequivocal commands of the First Amendment. Consequently, I do not believe that any federal agencies, including Congress and this Court, have power or authority to subordinate speech and press to what they think are 'more important interests.' The contrary notion is, in my judgement, court-made not constitution-made."

CENSORSHIP DEADLY ENEMY OF FREEDOM

"If, as it seems, we are on the way to national censorship, I think it timely to suggest again that there are grave doubts in my mind as to the desirability or constitutionality of this Court's becoming a Supreme Board of Censors—reading books and viewing television performances to determine whether, if permitted, they might adversely affect the morals of the people throughout the many diversified local communities in this vast country. It is true that the ordinance here is on its face only applicable to 'obscene or indecent writings.' It is also true that this particular kind of censorship is considered by many to be 'the obnoxious thing in its mildest and least repulsive form...' But illegitimate and unconstitutional practices get their first footing in that way...It is the duty of courts to be watchful for the constitutional rights of the citizen and against any stealthy encroachments thereon. While it is 'obscenity and indecency' before us today, the experience of mankind—both ancient and modern—shows that this type of elastic phrase can, and most likely will be synonymous with the political, and maybe with the religious unorthodoxy of tomorrow.

"Censorship is the deadly enemy of freedom and progress. The plain language of the Constitution forbids it. I protest against the judiciary giving it a foothold."

CONDEMNS HIGH-HANDEDNESS OF THOSE WHO PATROL NEWSSTANDS

Justice Douglas said that while he found the book in question repulsive 'neither this book nor its author or distributor can be punished under our Bill of Rights for publishing or distributing it.' In his opinion neither the courts nor legislatures have power to weigh the values of speech or utterances. According to Justice Douglas:

"Freedom of expression can be suppressed if, and to the extent that, it is so closely brigaded with illegal action as to be an inseparable part of it. As a people, we cannot afford to relax that standard. For the test that suppresses a cheap tract today can suppress a literary gem tomorrow. All it need do is to incite a lascivious thought or arouse a lustful desire. The list of books that judges or juries can place in that category is endless."

In agreeing that the ordinance was unconstitutional, Justice Douglas concluded: "What the Court does today may possibly provide some degree of safeguard to booksellers by making those who patrol bookstalls proceed less high-handedly than has been their custom."

BOOKSELLER ENTITLED TO PUT ON EXPERT WITNESSES

Justice Frankfurter, noticing that "There is an important difference in the scope of the power of a State to regulate what feeds the belly and what feeds the brain" agreed that the ordinance was unconstitutional. He also felt that the bookseller was denied due process when the court excluded the testimony of his expert witnesses. Justice Frankfurter said:

"The uncertainties pertaining to an obscenity prosecution and the speculative proof that the issue is likely to entail, are considerations that reinforce the right of one charged with obscenity—a right implicit in the very nature of the legal concept of obscenity—to enlighten the judgment of the tribunal, be it the jury or as in this case the judge, regarding the prevailing literary and moral community standards and to do so through qualified experts. It is immaterial whether the basis of the exclusion of such testimony is irrelevance, or the incompetence of experts, to testify to such matters. The two reasons coalesce, for community standards or the psychological or physiological consequences of questioned literature can as a matter of fact hardly be established except through experts. Therefore, to exclude such expert testimony goes to the very essence of the defense and therefore to the constitutional safeguards of due process."

SUBJECTIVE TASTE OF JUDGE OR JURY NOT TEST OF OBSCENITY

"There is no external measuring rod of obscenity. Neither, on the other hand, is its ascertainment a merely subjective reflection of the taste or moral outlook of individual jurors or individual judges. Since the law through its functionaries is 'applying contemporary community standards' in determining what constitutes obscenity, it surely must be deemed rational, and therefore relevant to the issue of obscenity to allow light to be shed on what those 'contemporary community standards' are. Their interpretation ought not to depend solely on the necessarily limited, hit-or-miss, subjective view of what they are believed to be by the individual juror or judge. It bears repetition that the determination of obscenity is for juror or judge not on the basis of his personal upbringing or restricted reflection or particular experience of life, but on the basis of 'contemporary community standards.' Can it be doubted that there is a great difference in what is to be deemed obscene in 1959 compared with what was deemed obscene in 1859?"

CONDEMNS EXCLUSION OF EVIDENCE ON COMMUNITY STANDARDS

Justice Harlan was reluctant to rule on the constitutionality of the ordinance. He held that the bookseller was denied due process of law because the trial court "turned aside every attempt...to introduce evidence bearing on community standards." Justice Harlan said:

"The Fourteenth Amendment does not permit a conviction unless the work complained of is found substantially to exceed the limits of candor set by contemporary community standards. The community cannot, where liberty of speech and press are at issue, condemn that which it generally tolerates. This being so, it follows that due process—using that term in its primary sense of an opportunity to be heard and to defend a substantive right—requires a State to allow a litigant in some manner to introduce proof on this score.

"In my opinion, this conviction is fatally defective in that the trial judge, as I read the record, turned aside every attempt by appellant to introduce evidence bearing on community standards. The exclusionary rulings were not limited to offered expert testimony. This had the effect of depriving appellant of the opportunity to offer any proof on a constitutionally relevant issue."